PRAISE FOR THE *CRIMSON THREAD*

Educational, mysterious, spiritual, the *Crimson Thread* will capture the imagination of teenagers better than any video game!

—*Allen J. Huth,* president,
Ezra Project and Gideons International

From the opening pages of the *Crimson Thread*, you are drawn into an adventure that is both fictional and factual. The story will intrigue you and leave you contemplating its truths. It is a great read!

—*Pastor George Morrison,* pastor emeritus
and founder of Truth and Life Ministries

the
crimson
thread

the
crimson
thread

TAPESTRY OF TIME SERIES

❦ BOOK ONE ❦

BRAD PELSUE

the
crimson
thread

Copyright © 2020 by Brad Pelsue

Scripture taken from the New King James Version®. Copyright © 1982 by Thomas Nelson. Used by permission. All rights reserved.

The views and opinions expressed in this book are those of the author and do not necessarily reflect the official policy or position of Illumify Media Global.

Published by
Illumify Media Global
www.IllumifyMedia.com
"We bring your book to life!"

Library of Congress Control Number: 2020922933

Paperback ISBN: 978-1-949021-68-4
eBook ISBN: 978-1-949021-69-1

Typeset by Art Innovations (http://artinnovations.in/)
Cover design by Debbie Lewis

Printed in the United States of America

*For my Grandchildren,
Chloe, Isabel, Reid, Alli, Sophia, and Alexandria.
And their parents, Sarah and Tom, Joel and Michelle.*

*Most of all, thanks to my wife, Georgi, who has taken this journey
with me. She has been my first reader and my most gracious critic.
Thanks to my editors and coaches, who pushed me to see things
in new lights, and helped me weave the tapestry's stories together.
Thanks also to my friends who listened to my stories on motorcycle
rides, band breaks and many excursions into the Word. A special
shout out to Ron, Leo and Mongo.*

CONTENTS

SACRIFICE | AD 33 | JERUSALEM

REVELATION

RESTORATION

Map of the World as it was Known in Ancient Times

Map of Israel, Ancient And Modern

LEGEND OF THE TAPESTRY

c. AD 1401

]I
INVASION

Cappadocia

"They're coming, Papop," Agour called out to his grandfather. "Their army is kicking up a huge dust cloud."

He was barely fifteen but considered himself a seasoned warrior. A bit small for his age, he had a wiry build, dark eagle eyes that could see in the distance better than most, and he could run like the wind.

Rumors of the advancing Mongol army had reached his village two weeks ago. Now, from his position on the heights above the cave cliffs and the fairy-candle rock formations, an icy chill went through his veins.

How long will it be until their army gets to our village? he thought. *It doesn't matter. The camel caravans warned us. We cannot prevail against the army of Timur. We are just villagers.*

Timur was ruthless. He was descended from the Mongol conqueror Genghis Kahn. He had destroyed the great armies of India and Persia, and now his army was invading this part of the Silk Road.

"I remember your stories, Papop," Agour reminded his grandfather, "how thousands of our people hid underground in

Dikuyu and survived Alexander the Great, the Persians, and the others."

"Yes, and we will again," Papop assured Agour.

The villagers of Cappadocia were farmers and they got their news at the market. Usually the buzz was about tomatoes, garlic, and arugula. Sometimes it was apples or pumpkins, and always it was about the weather.

Today was very different. Fear was in every conversation.

Death and destruction will arrive soon enough, Agour thought, feeling it in his bones.

He watched as the elders of the village gathered around Papop. *Are the rumors true?* Everybody wanted to know.

"Dikuyu has always kept its people safe," Papop declared. "But we don't know enough about this army yet. Someone must get close enough to find out about their numbers, archers, cavalry, and, if possible, their weaknesses."

"There is no doubt they will pillage our land and worse," a voice called out from the gathering crowd. "They say killing is like a sport to Timur. He likes to watch people die."

Papop's eyes flashed at the man, and he raised his voice to be sure that all of the villagers could hear him. "Let us harvest what we can. Try to fill our storehouses. Bake bread. Store wine. Gather the animals."

There were nine underground levels in Dikuyu. Papop had taught Agour about all of them, even how to repair the cavernous water-storage cisterns at the lowest level. No one could go there except during the dry season before the rains came and filled them up.

In Dikuyu there was a place for everything. Food and wine was stored on the third level. Their unique flatbread would keep for a year. Sheep, goats, and chickens were kept in the stables. A church between the third and fourth levels was ornately carved from the volcanic rock.

Papop turned his gaze back to the elders. "Who will go?" he asked.

Agour sat silently between his best friend and his sister, but his mind was racing.

"Who will go?" Papop repeated. This time he raised his voice a bit to be sure the growing crowd heard him.

Silence.

Agour stared at the ground, then heard himself speak. "I will go," his voice waivered, "and Stefanos will go with me."

Did I really mean to say that? Agour thought.

"We will go," he repeated. His voice was stronger, and he looked directly at Papop. Not only had he said it, but he had dragged his best friend into what might be the last thing they would ever do. "We are small and quick and can get up close."

They were quick, for sure, and dependable. Papop and the elders had trained them well to throw spears and knives. They had killed deer and bears. They had killed wolves with their slingshots to protect their herds.

Papop turned to Agour and flashed *that* look.

Fear was on every face. Nobody dared let their eyes meet Papop's. *He has volunteers,* the onlookers thought.

Papop quietly turned back to the lads. "Are you sure?" he asked, longing for a different answer.

They couldn't back out now. They were all in. "We will go," Agour insisted. Stefanos turned his soft blue eyes to look directly at Agour and nodded resolutely. His bravery increased when he said it. "We can get up close."

Stefanos paused a moment and thought, *What did I just get into?* But it was too late. He was committed.

Suddenly, a sharp elbow struck Agour's ribs. "Don't do anything stupid," Phebe whispered.

His sister Phebe was full of life. Like Agour, she had a slight build and was very quick. With light brown hair and hazel eyes, she had a gracious look about her. Her voice was as gentle as the rest of her features, until she said, "And try to get all the facts, not like you did last—"

"Thanks!" Agour snapped, cutting her off.

Papop rose and addressed the assembly. "It is set now. While Agour and Stefanos are gone, we will store up everything we can, just as our ancestors did. Follow the ancient plan. When the lads return, we will release the giant millstone door and close off the entrance. The invaders will not find any trace of us."

When Papop turned to the young warriors, he said the most frightening thing ever. "If you do not return before the army arrives, we will be forced to seal the entrance. You will be on your own. Make sure nobody follows you. Do not even let them see you, and when you return, do not leave tracks or traces that might guide anyone here."

Agour nodded as he tightened his kilt around his waist and tugged at the leather strap on his sandals. Stefanos did the same. They reached their fingers into the dirt and rubbed it on their shirts to make their own desert camouflage.

"Come here, lads, and turn around," Papop said. He rubbed dirt on the backs of their shirts. Then he turned them around and applied a little more dirt on their shoulders and looked deep into their eyes.

Agour reached up, removed his red headband and handed it to Papop. Stefanos did the same. "These would make us too visible," Agour said. As the lads attached their slingshots, swords, and knives to their belts and grasped their spears, Agour noticed sadness in his grandfather's eyes.

Papop took each by a shoulder and turned them around quickly to face their mission. "Godspeed," he said, gently tapping their backs as he commissioned them.

Stefanos, who had always been a strong runner, took the lead, setting a loping pace they could maintain for miles. Each of them had a small leather flask filled with water slung over his shoulder and a pouch that held an apple and a handful of pumpkin seeds. They would have to find more food and water as they went.

The lads stuck to the high bluffs so they could look down on Timur's encampment without being visible. Agour and Stefanos could see the rows and rows of archers and spearmen. There were thousands of horses, and soldiers, beyond counting. They stories about the magnificent and powerful bows made of wood, bone, and horn layered together. The arrows flew farther than they had ever seen. It only augmented their fear.

"This army will never be defeated," Agour exclaimed. "But Papop already knows that. Still, we must get closer to see what they are really like."

Throughout the night, Agour and Stefanos took turns watching the fires flickering beside the thousands of tents. It was terrifying to think of what might happen to their village and the many other villages in this great Anatolian plain. Would they be safe inside Dikuyu? Only time would tell, but Agour was beginning to doubt it.

"These Mongols never sleep," Stefanos muttered. "Fires burn all night, and sentries move throughout the camp. Remember to keep your head down."

When morning came, horsemen could be seen riding ten abreast while the soldiers practiced their swordsmanship.

"Look how far the arrows fly," Stefanos said. "It's true about their bows."

Agour and Stefanos descended into the valley. They darted behind rocks and the few trees they could find. As the day ended, they hid in the lengthening shadows.

"Stop," Agour grunted, putting his hand out to restrain Stefanos. By now they had come to the edge of the Red River and were crouching in the reeds and willows. "Those are the sentinels," Agour whispered, pointing across the river.

Then they heard it. "ooOOIIAAAAhhhaa!" The otherworldly wail was terrifying. Agour and Stefanos had never heard anything like it. It was a sound that penetrated their bones.

"ooOOIIAAAAhhhaa!" The monstrous beasts trumpeted an unearthly sound, shaking the ground as they walked. Each was clad with a metal mask to protect its head and a shining breastplate. A wooden box-like fortress was cinched high on the back of each beast. The creatures had become mobile fortresses, with drivers standing at the front of the box, and two—or sometimes four—archers in the corners. The archers were firing down on their victims and then ducking below the rim, even while the beast was advancing.

Agour and Stefanos could not believe their eyes.

The behemoths had giant tusks protruding from each side of their mouths. The ends of the tusks had been sawed off, and giant sword-like metal blades were attached in their place. The monsters appeared to have five legs. The fifth leg extended from its face. Agour watched a leg swing side to side across the ground. A moment later, the giant trunk that he had thought was a leg grasped some straw and swung it up to its mouth and fed itself.

They watched with unbelieving eyes when a captured soldier from a conquered army was brought out. He was given a spear and ordered to fight the animal.

There's no way his spear could hurt that beast, Agour observed. *It could never penetrate its hide, much less its armor.*

The soldier tried to defend himself until the metal blades on the tusks penetrated his midsection. The monster lifted him up and threw him into the air. Blood spewed everywhere. As the creature turned again to attack the lifeless body, Agour and Stefanos fought the urge to hurl what little was left in their stomachs. They did not dare make a sound.

This was the beast from Hell. Agour knew it for sure. He wanted to run, but he knew he could not. In fact, he could not even breathe. They crouched still lower to the ground.

"Two hundred?" Agour guessed at the number of monsters. Stefanos nodded and swallowed hard.

"How many archers do you think there are?" Agour asked.

"Th-thousands," Stefanos stuttered. "Maybe even ten thousand, plus spearmen and foot soldiers. It's like a whole city on the warpath."

The spies retreated from the river's edge. They found a new perch from which to observe another fearsome sight. The army deployed a floating bridge. First, a small boat stretched two huge ropes across the river. Then teams of horses appeared in the distance drawing giant barges with wheels. One after another, the teams of horses waded into the water until the barge began to float. Soldiers secured the barges together and anchored the ropes. Once the horses had climbed back onto the shore, they joined the rest of the army as it crossed over the river and headed south toward Dikuyu.

After the soldiers came the aptly named camp followers. They were the ragtags of the earth. They would beg, steal, or scare the locals out of their goods and sell them to the soldiers. They were wanderers, yet sometimes they were the wives and children of the soldiers. They gathered food and scavenged the land, and after Timur's victories, they gleaned what plunder the army might have missed.

When the evening fires began to glow, soldiers came out to visit the camp followers. Before long, the area was bustling with the aroma of fresh cakes and the sizzle of roasting animals that had been confiscated from nearby farmers. Some enterprising followers sold beer.

Above the din of the camp, the lilting call of a lone flute rose. Soon it was joined by a small bagpipe and a tambourine.

Songs began to regale the triumphs of Timur and his mighty warriors. The fires were surrounded by exuberant folk dancing and singing.

Stefanos and Agour crept closer. When they flattened themselves against the ground, they felt the droning pipes reverberate in their chests.

"That's Timur," Stefanos whispered, pointing to the man they had seen earlier. "See how he walks with a limp. They call him Timur the Lame."

"Ah," Agour whispered. "Sounds like Tam-er-lane. That's him."

Finally, they got close enough to hear a deep, raspy voice speaking a language they could not understand. "Bagduddi" and "Damaskees" was all they could make out.

"That sounds like *Baghdad* and *Damascus*. So that is where they are going. They will follow the valley right through our village."

Suddenly a small child came running from the direction of the celebration. He ran out of the camp and right into the arms of Agour; whose veins turned to ice. He cupped his hand over the child's mouth and pulled him to the ground. His body muffled any sound and prevented him from squirming.

For a while the three lay motionless in the shadows. The boy, finally subdued, appeared to be no more than three years old.

"Leave him," Stefanos whispered. "We got the info. Let's go."

"If I let him go, he will scream," whispered Agour. "And they will surely capture us."

Agour kept the child's mouth covered and motioned with his free hand to Stefanos. Stealthily, the lads carried the boy away from the encampment.

"Whew, that was close," sighed Stefanos when he thought they were out of earshot. "Let him go now."

"No, we can't do that." Agour was calculating the consequences. "If we let him go, the hyenas or the owls will get him, and his blood will be on our hands."

Suddenly a young woman's voice pierced the night air and rose above the merriment of the camp followers. "That sounded like some kind of banshee," said Stefanos.

As soon as he heard it, the boy perked up. He wiggled right out of Agour's grip and started running back to the camp.

"Let him go!" Stefanos insisted.

"No." In a few steps Agour recaptured the child and covered his mouth again. "As long as no one knows about us, they will think he just wandered off. We are well beyond any search area. We must take him with us."

The night was now their friend as they ran across the flat plain back toward their home. Stefanos made a sling out of his shirt. It was big enough to hold the child, and the constant motion of the running rocked him to sleep as they ran.

Stefanos and Agour used the stars to navigate until the clouds gathered, obscuring all but the crescent moon that peeked through from time to time. They passed the child back and forth as they scaled the ridgeline.

"Stop a moment," gasped Agour, with his hands on his knees and the boy in the sling dangling from his neck.

The glow of campfires was no longer visible. All Agour and Stefanos knew was that this violent army would use its powerful war beasts to break through Dikuyu's defenses. The millstone door had never faced this kind of power.

"Let's go," Stefanos insisted. "Cold winds are kicking up from the northwest. This is never good." As the boys ran back along the ridgeline, it began to rain. Gentle at first, it soon transformed into a full-on harvest gale, pelting them as they strained into the wind.

Not now, thought Agour as he looked up to heaven. The child had just awakened and he was hungry. His cries drowned out any other goal Agour and Stefanos thought they had. They could make it back without more food, but now they had to waste precious time to feed this little monster whom they had now named Seymour.

"I know Papop always says we need the rain in this dry land, but not now. We have to get back." The young warriors struggled in the rainy darkness to find something they could give him to eat. As they ran, the ground softened under their feet and turned into mud.

"This is a farmer's field," Agour said. "Somewhere there is food." Knowing the harvest was over, the pair struggled in the darkness and mud to find gleanings the farmers might have missed. Finally, Agour stepped on one small squash, which he quickly cleaned and cut up with his knife; then he gave its nutritious contents to Seymour. It was perfect timing and kept him quiet.

"Move!" Stefanos whispered. "Something is out there." He took the lead while Agour lifted their small charge, throwing the sling over his shoulder. Seymour drifted off to sleep again, aided by Agour's steady stride.

Eventually they eluded whatever it was . . .

In the darkness, Agour wondered about his future: *What will happen to my family? Will there be enough food stored up in Dikuyu? Papop and Grandmother are too old to run away. Will they just die there? Will there be anything left of their village? What will happen to the Tapestry the family has protected for centuries?*

The Tapestry was magnificent and ancient. Something about it seemed to be alive. *How can I protect it? What if Timur should find it? That is unthinkable!*

Dawn was just breaking when they finally arrived back at the entrance to Dikuyu. Seymour was hungry again, but Agour just handed his sling, child, and belongings to one of the village women. She was startled but eventually accepted the lad and began feeding him some nuts and raisins from her pouch while she followed the crowd.

Dikuyu was prepared for disaster. Huge ceramic containers called amphorae were filled with grains, seeds, and wine and then sealed with wax. These provisions could remain in the cool, dry caves for decades and still be nourishing. "What's amazing about seeds," Papop would say, "is that they are both food for now and provision for the future. If you don't eat them now, you can plant them later, and they will feed many people."

A chill went through Agour's body when he rounded a corner and saw Papop standing at the entrance to the underground city. The weight of Seymour had been heavy on his neck, but the weight of his message about Timur was even heavier.

Thousands of frightened farmers and villagers compressed into the narrow tunnels. Timur would never imagine that so many people could just disappear below ground.

Caves also pocked the surrounding mountainsides. Multitudes of them had been hand dug over centuries in the volcanic tuff, spewed from distant Mt. Ercyges. The soft rock was easy to dig and made perfect homes and hideouts.

Agour and Stefanos had expended their last ounce of energy by the time they reached Papop. The lads took turns telling him everything they had seen and heard.

"They even have five-legged beasts with swords for tusks," Agour said. "They will surely kill us all, if they find us."

When the village woman arrived carrying Seymour, the child was crying from fear and hunger. Agour was in no mood to help,

but he needed to explain to Papop what had happened and why
they had carried the boy back with them.

"Look at his clothing, said Phebe. "The fringe on his jacket is
woven with bright colors and strange symbols. His cap has ridges
in it like a crown. And just look at his boot. It comes up almost
to his knee. This cannot be the child of a soldier or a peasant. This
is the child of an important man. Maybe even a son of Timur."

"Where is his other boot?" Phebe whispered. "What if
Timur's army finds it? It could lead them right to us. Talk about
doing something stupid."

How could he have lost it? Agour thought, mentally retracing
his steps, but he couldn't recall where it could be.

Papop quickly rose to his feet and pointed to the entrance.
"Inside!" he commanded. The subterranean cave network would
be their home until the invaders had passed.

He flashed a helpless look at Agour and Stefanos. "Timur
is headed this way, and he will surely be searching for the boy.
Dikuyu is about to face its greatest test," he said.

Papop looked into fearful eyes and lovingly pressed the
people forward. Some of them tried to hug him, but he would
not allow it. "Keep moving. It will be okay," he repeated again
and again.

When all of the villagers were inside, Agour, Stefanos, and
Papop went in.

The millstone door weighed over a thousand pounds and
was held in place by a small, angular stone chock. Using a lever,
the boys were able to nudge the millstone just enough for Papop
to reach down and removed the chock stone. "Stand clear,"
he called out.

Agour started to feel they had just boarded the *Ark of Doom*.

The cavernous city reverberated with the sound of the
giant rolling millstone. It could be heard through the speaking

tubes and ventilation shafts. It crashed into its resting place, and the echo could be felt in their bones. The villagers were safely sealed in, and Dikuyu's millstone door was now their strongest protector.

For most of his life, Papop had told the stories of survival by the ancestors in this city.

But could they survive Timur?

2

ESCAPE

Cappadocia

*A*drenaline was still coursing through Agour's body, and his mind was racing: *Now we sit here, waiting for the Mongols to kill us. We are trapped.* It took a few minutes for the new reality to sink in. The echo from the millstone dissipated, leaving the sound of people and livestock jostling through caverns that were lit only by a few candles and oil lamps.

Agour's heart pounded. His thoughts raged within him. He was now kicking himself as he thought, *The caravans were right about Timur. He is pure evil. He kills because he enjoys it.*

"We will all be slaughtered," Agour whispered to his father Andros and to Papop. "This place is not safe anymore. We have to get out!"

"It is too late," Papop insisted in his best hold your horses tone of voice. "The millstone door will remain closed until the threat passes. We will be safe. You will see." Papop led the way down the labyrinth of ladders and stone stairways that had been cut into the rock centuries ago.

Agour drew Papop close and whispered, "You do not know the giant war beasts of Timur. They tear people apart. We have seen it."

The main gathering place inside Dikuyu was the cave church. Its carved-out walls were smoothly finished with ivory-colored plaster and ornately painted with scenes from the Bible. On the inside, its appearance rivaled churches in Rome, Constantinople, and Jerusalem, except there were no windows. The only light came from oil lamps and candles flickering in the nooks and niches. It was carved in the traditional shape of the cross. Overhead, the domed ceiling presented an intricate painting of the resurrection of Jesus.

The church had not changed much for the past five hundred years. There had never been seating. Agour and his sister Phebe stood with the congregation. They fidgeted while the priest prayed for everyone's safety. *Please, God, keep us hidden from Timur.* Nobody really listened after that.

Despair flooded Agour. He couldn't shake it. His mind raced with fear: *We are trapped like sitting ducks. The priest is talking about the body and blood of Jesus, but I'm worried about my own body and blood.*

And then there was the matter of Seymour, the boy he had carried from Timur's camp. People were beginning to talk.

"Look at his fancy clothing," a villager had said. "When they find his other boot, Timur will surely come looking for him."

A shrill woman's voice pierced the air, "Why did Agour bring him back here? He has put us all at risk."

Getting twenty thousand people underground in Dikuyu wasn't easy, but for Papop the challenge was to keep them all quiet. The command for silence was issued, and people waited.

On the third day the ground started to vibrate. Thousands of soldiers were passing right over Dikuyu, unaware of the civilization below.

Phebe took hold of her brother and trembled as the stomping of soldiers' feet gave way to the ominous rumble of the elephants. Suddenly the sound stopped. Timur was directly above them.

I need to get out of here now! Agour thought. His heart screamed. *These people will kill me before Timur ever gets a chance.*

Agour continued to press his grandfather. "Papop, there has to be another way out, or this will be our grave."

Papop considered the options and then said softly, "I will help you." He put his hand on Agour's shoulder. "But before we do anything, we have to protect the Tapestry."

Nobody knew how long the Tapestry had hung in the church. According to the legend, it had power to "communicate" with many who learned its stories. To those who took the time to focus on the pictures and symbols, it held special properties that conveyed wisdom and strength. There was even talk that it was like a veil that guarded access to another realm where someone could look beyond this present world and into something far greater. Sometimes people were healed, and others were helped in their struggle against the dark forces.

Some called it a "thin place."

When Papop married Grandma Phebe, her family had already been custodians of the Tapestry for generations. Then it became their obligation together. Now they gazed at the legendary object as if they were being forced to hide a member of their own family. Centuries of stories flashed through Papop's mind. *It isn't just the caves; it is the Tapestry that protected our ancestors*, he thought.

The tremor of horses and elephants continued overhead. "They will never get past the millstone, even if they find it," Papop declared. "But we cannot take the risk that our Tapestry could fall into the hands of Timur."

The Tapestry was slightly more than a yard in width, and maybe two yards tall.

The priest silently lifted the golden rod that suspended it and handed one end to Papop. He instructed Agour and Phebe to hold the bottom end. "Just hold it. Don't pull."

Phebe touched the fabric. "Did you feel that?"

Agour nodded. He felt it too. It made him feel safe, even protected.

The Tapestry displayed the same stories as the scenes on the walls of the church. Eden, The Ten Commandments, Passover, Mary and Jesus in the manger, Christ on the Cross, and several others.

Agour and Phebe held the small pomegranate-colored tassels at the bottom corners. They watched while Papop and the priest rolled the Tapestry and wrapped it.

"Agour," Papop said, "find a container that will hold this."

Agour left quickly and returned before long, carrying an earthen cylinder. It was flat on the bottom with carrying handles on the shoulders of the jar. When he emptied the vessel, a few pumpkin seeds fell out. He quickly stuffed them into the small pouch at his waist and wiped the jar as clean as he could. The priest and Papop slid the tapestry into the cylinder and placed the cap on top.

"Bring some of those candles," Papop instructed, pointing to the altar.

Papop and the priest slowly turned the cylinder while Agour and Phebe dribbled the candle wax to seal the cap.

"Did you feel that? The elephants are battering the millstone. We are all doomed," Agour cried out. The sound of the tusks scraping against the millstone echoed through the airshafts and passageways. "Let's get going!"

"One more thing," Papop continued as Agour rolled his eyes. "Grab hold of the other handle." Together they lifted the jar and started down to the lower levels of Dikuyu. Their whole family and Stefanos followed.

"Where are we going?"

"Down! To the cisterns." Papop instructed, pointing his finger. "It is your only way out."

"Your?" Agour questioned. "Aren't we all going together?"

"The rest of us must stay here. No matter what," Papop said definitively. "No discussion."

At the underground stables, Papop stopped. "Here," he said, indicating a smaller millstone that was poised to seal off the livestock. Together, Agour and Papop lifted the clay jar and gently positioned it behind the millstone so that no one would see it. "Leave it," said Papop. "We will come back and cover it with plaster."

"Let's get going," Agour beckoned to Stefanos, who looked away and did not answer. He was still shaking from the reconnaissance trip. His eyes told everything. There was no way he was going to leave the safety of this cave and risk being caught. Words were not necessary.

"Okay then," Agour said, releasing his lifetime friend. "I need to get going."

"I will go." It was the voice of Phebe. She was clear and resolute. The family stopped cold and turned to the girl standing beside her brother.

"No, Phebe!" said Andros, their father. "Your mother and I will not allow it."

"Indeed!" her mother, Adrianna, chimed in. "What are you thinking?"

"But I *want* to go," she insisted. Phebe was thirteen, and she was determined. "I do not want to die in this cave. If Agour wants to go, I want to go. Besides, I have heard from the caravans about many places that would be safer than this dark cave."

Papop turned to his family. His eyes were heavy, and he was resolved. He knelt down on one knee and looked into the face of Phebe and then up to Agour. Rising, he placed his arms on the shoulders of his grandchildren.

"Agour has seen things we have not imagined," Papop began. "We will not prevent him from following his heart. And we will not prevent Phebe from joining him on this journey. We cannot know what is before them, but we know their beautiful hearts. They will leave a great emptiness in all of us. Yet, we must release them. No, we will *send* them. They will go into a larger world. Our Dikuyu has served us well. And if perchance we do not survive, they will be the remnants who will tell our story to future generations."

Everybody was weeping as Papop concluded his speech.

Adrianna embraced her daughter, then held her shoulders and gave her a lengthy once-over. "You cannot go looking like a girl. It will be safer for you if everyone thinks you are brothers."

She produced some clothing that Agour had outgrown and fitted her daughter. Phebe also donned a shepherd's headscarf, tunic, and sandals. They were ready.

"Alright then," said Papop. "You must go now."

The cacaphony of Timur's army continued echoing through the caves above. Agour turned to Papop. "The Tapestry," he said, "will not be safe here. We need to take it."

"No!" There was no discussion. The baritone voice of their father had spoken. "You may go, my son, and Phebe, as she chooses. But the Tapestry is bulky, and you cannot carry it through the cisterns. If it were to get wet, it would drown you both. When you come back," Andros said, "you know where it is. Maybe you will tell your descendants."

THE DESCENT

THERE were several shafts where the inhabitants of Dikuyu could draw water from the cisterns all the way to the top levels. Papop stopped at the closest one. "We will lower you into this cistern using the well bucket."

Papop knelt down, took a stick, and began drawing a map on the floor. "This is the only way. Remember, these cisterns are designed to collect as much runoff water as possible from the hills around us. Since it has been raining, all of the watercourses and conduits will be nearly full. Whenever you have a chance, take a deep breath, do it! It might save your life. Don't forget that water always flows downhill. If you are *not* going against the flow, you are going the wrong way. No mistakes. Your lives depend upon doing this right. There is a large conduit here"—he tapped the map with the stick—"and you will hear the water rushing in. When you come to places where the conduits grow smaller, always take the largest one."

To each of them he presented a small reed tube. "This is to breathe with when the water rises," he said. "There is no light and the water is deep. Be sure your intake is above the water's surface."

Adrianna carefully rolled three small woven kilims and loaded them into a leather pouch made from the stomach of a sheep. Then she produced a little gold coin bearing the image of the Emperor Justinian. It had been given as part of her dowry and was already centuries old. She sealed it into the pouch using bitumen and wax.

"That will keep the water out," she said as she presented it to her daughter. "You can trade these when you get to Constantinople. Go to the Great Agora. Any weaver there will recognize our style of images, patterns, and knots—and our quality. The kilim on the bottom is the small replica of our Tapestry of Time. It will serve you well. The coin has been in our family for centuries. Keep it always. Pass it down. Do not sell it unless your life depends on it."

Papop embraced Agour and Phebe. He kissed them each on the cheeks. Then he held them away from him by their shoulders, looked proudly into their eyes, and said, "Go, now."

Agour stood strong and resolute. Grandma Phebe tied a rope around the waist of her namesake granddaughter. She showed the other end to Agour. "Tie this to your wrist once Phebe gets into the cistern. It will keep you together."

"Be strong, my children. When you come out at the springs, rejoice. God will have truly shined upon you," Papop stated.

THE CISTERNS

AGOUR sat down on top of the well bucket, which was a wood frame with a bag made of animal skin laced to it. As a final goodbye, Stefanos took hold of the crank and lowered his friend, then Phebe into the lightless underground water supply.

The pair had imagined an easy departure, but this was going to be the most difficult thing they had ever done. For starters, Agour was not a good swimmer. As soon as he dropped into the cistern, he was over his head, flailing to find the sidewall, fearing he might drown before Phebe even got there.

Phebe was much better in the water. Once she was lowered into the cistern, Agour tied Phebe's cord to his wrist, and the pair paddled toward the sound of the inlet, always with one hand on the sidewall as Papop had instructed.

Agour promised himself that he would not drown and leave his body to decompose and poison the water supply of Dikuyu. *No way. We will make it,* he decreed.

The sound of water rushing into the cistern guided them. Derek boosted Phebe into the flow of the aqueduct. Their knees and hands scraped on the rough clay pipes, as they strained against the rushing water. *Take a breath every time you can,* Papop's words replayed in their minds as they spat out the runoff water.

With a giant push they reached the second cistern. A small vent above them let in a glimmer of light. They felt hopeful. Their hands groped for the sidewalls as they made their way around the perimeter toward the roaring water falling from three inlet pipes.

"Take the middle one," Phebe repeated Papop's words. "We are still on course."

Together they tried to position themselves to climb into the aqueduct. Agour was flailing at the water, trying to stay afloat, while boosting his sister up to the inlet tubes.

Phebe strained to get a good hold, but she opened her mouth at just the wrong time. Losing her grip, she was flushed back into the cistern, just over Agour's head. Her momentum tightened the rope, dragging them both away from the wall.

I have to make it! he told himself, forcing his way to the surface and gasping for air. *It can't end this way.*

On the second try, Agour was able to boost Phebe into the middle duct. With the water rushing against her, she gained a foothold. The rope gnawed at her waist as Agour pulled himself out of the cistern. Again, Papop's words came back to them: *If you are not going against the flow, you are going the wrong way.*

The final conduit ended at the base of a small, spring-fed pond. Using the breathing tubes Papop had supplied, they hid beneath the surface in a clump of reeds and waited.

Cautiously, Agour climbed to the rim of the pond. Startled by a shadow, he quickly dropped below the waterline.

A flash of thought went through him: *Papop? Is he even alive? Did the war elephants break through the millstone? What about Grandma Phebe, Mother, Dad, and Stefanos? What about the Tapestry? We made it,* he thought. *He would be proud of us.*

Eventually a goat walked up to the pond and drank. Agour and Phebe decided it was safe enough. Pulling themselves up by branches, they collapsed along the bank. Muddy, soaked, scraped, and bruised, they finally escaped the darkness.

Phebe cautiously checked her pouch. The precious weavings were still dry.

Constantinople, the Capitol of the Empire was ahead of them.

And . . . they were free.

3

CONSTANTINOPLE

Capital of the Empire

*A*gour looked up at the crescent moon. The last time he had seen that, he was running with Stefanos, and Seymour around his neck. After the cisterns, most of the past month was spent on the Silk Road working as camel pullers, in the caravans. Finally Phebe and Agour gazed across the waters of the Bosphorus at Constantinople, the Eastern Capitol of the Roman Empire.

"Timur could never conquer this," Phebe declared. "Just look at the city walls. They are invincible. What's more, water almost completely surrounds it."

On the highest hill, dominating the skyline, stood the largest building Phebe had ever seen. "Hagia Sofia." Phebe sighed. "Remember what Grandma Phebe told us? The artwork on the walls is like the stories in our Tapestry. I want to see it!"

"Of course," Agour replied, "but first we have to get across the water on one of those sailboats."

"I can't believe the caravaneer didn't even pay us enough to get across," Phebe protested. "Will we have to sell one of our kilims to pay the ferryman?"

"Let me try something first," Agour said. He had learned the art of bartering in the market of Dikuyu and honed his skills in the caravan.

Phebe watched her brother saunter up to the ferryman and gesture across the water. She only recognized a few words. After haggling for what seemed like forever, Agour turned and motioned to his sister to come down to a boat.

"Get in," he directed. "I have joined the crew for today to pay for our passage."

"You have never even seen a boat like this," Phebe whispered. "How did you convince him you could sail?"

"Easy," Agour replied. "He talked. I nodded and he heard what he wanted to hear. After all, you and I were camel pullers in the caravans; how hard could this be? It's just a ferry trip. Get in," he repeated anxiously. "I will release these ropes and jump in at the last moment."

The ferry was loaded with bags of grain and glazed jars full of wine and spices that reminded Phebe of the Tapestry hidden in Dikuyu. Agour cast off the dock line and jumped into the boat. The ferry wobbled as the huge triangular sail caught the wind.

"Pull!" cried the ferryman. Agour did not understand the language of his new boss at all. "Pull!" the ferryman repeated, pointing to the rope of the main sail.

Agour grabbed the line and tugged on it. The sail tightened and the tiny ferry surged forward. Once Agour thought he had gotten the knack, he decided on his own to snug the sail a little more, which increased the wind pressure nearly capsizing the boat. The ferryman yelled strange foreign words that any sailor could clearly understand. He was found out.

Never mind, he thought. *We are on our way.*

Phebe felt a thrill. For the past month she had been thankful that her mother had given her Agour's old clothes to disguise her as a boy. Now she removed her bandana. Her dark hair billowed in the wind, and her hazel eyes and broad smile glistened in the reflections of the sun on the water. Her masquerade was over. She was Phebe, and she was in Constantinople.

When they reached the dock, Agour stepped onto the stone wharf and secured the bow line. Quickly, he helped his sister ashore, waved to the ferryman, and the two disappeared into the throngs of dockworkers, passengers, and panhandlers headed through the city gates. For a moment they stopped and looked back across the Bosporus strait. They thought of their family huddled in Dikuyu. *Are they even alive?*

"No!" Shouted Phebe as she clutched her bag. She glared at a boy who had tried to steal it. "Go!" she yelled at him, tightening her grip on the small pouch.

"Let go!" Agour yelled, pivoting and slugging the would-be thief, who finally released his grip and fled.

Along the great harbor, they paused to look at the ships. Flags from everywhere in the Empire rippled in the wind. Alexandria in Egypt. Caesarea in Judea. Athens . . . Rome . . . Carthage in Africa, and the Crimea in Russia. The seamen shouted out to one another, but Agour and Phebe understood none of it.

"This way," Phebe tugged Agour's shirt. Together they followed the merchants through the massive iron gates into the city.

"The guards do not look friendly. Keep going," Phebe insisted.

Once inside, their heads pivoted wildly as they tried to get their bearings and figure out what to do next.

"Maybe we can find work here," Phebe suggested.

"Maybe," Agour responded.

Wandering the streets, they suddenly came upon the huge building they had seen from across the water. The Hagia Sophia, which was also known as the Church of Holy Wisdom. It was nearly square at the base and almost as large as a football field. The white dome glistened brightly above every other building. For over eight hundred years, it had already stood watching over the Queen City of the Empire.

"People in the caravan talked about it," gushed Phebe. "Some said the dome appeared to be suspended from heaven. "

Agour held his breath as he and his sister entered through the highest doors they had ever imagined and into the sanctuary covered by the largest dome in the world. It was so majestic they could feel it.

Phebe quietly opened her pouch and withdrew their prized kilim. She held it up to compare it with mosaics on the walls and glass windows. "There! Look," she repeated over and over to Agour as she matched the depictions of Eden, Moriah, Gethsemane, Mt. Sinai and Passover. There was Rahab escaping Jericho by the red cord, and Jesus on the cross. In the center of the dome overhead was the golden depiction of the resurrected Jesus.

Agour broke the silence. "Quick, hide the kilim. We must find lodging. Let's go to the Bazaar and find a weaver like Grandmother Phebe told us."

AGORA, The Market

THE Great Agora was a bazaar on a scale the earth would not find elsewhere for centuries. People from everywhere in the world bought and sold here. Aromas of foods from India, Asia, and Spain wafted through the air. There were chess games from Persia, wheat and corn from Egypt, and armaments from Anatolia. Textiles from Persia and Afghanistan and prized silks from China were all on display.

As the daylight faded, the Agora was lit only by torches

in its narrow passageways and Aladdin-like oil lamps lit the shops.

"Where are the weavers?" Phebe asked. One of the shopkeepers slowly extended his hand toward a row of shops, then signaled quickly with his finger to turn to the right.

She thanked him, not knowing whether he understood or not.

At the end of the lane, they turned a corner to find the rug makers and weavers were all together. "There must be fifty shops," Phebe exclaimed. "Now what?"

A riot of patterns and colors beckoned them from each shop while the shopkeepers tried their best to draw them in.

"This just doesn't feel right," Phebe said. "Are we in the right place?"

Derek just shook his head and continued meandering from shop to shop.

"It is getting late," she warned. "Shops are closing. Where do we go?"

Rounding a corner, they saw a tiny shop where an old weaver sat on a very low bench. Her shop was piled high with old carpets of every color and size. A pattern called a Kartun, hung above her work.

She wore a white dress with a red sash, a traditional red bandana on her head, and peasant sandals. Her amber eyes were soft, and her broad smile was gentle.

The weaver halted her shuttle and slowly rose from her low bench, greeting her new arrivals. They perused her unusual goods for a brief time and were about to leave when they heard her voice call to them.

"Tea?" the hunched over woman asked, craning her neck to greet her visitors.

"Yes, please," said Agour, hoping there would be more than

tea. It did not occur to them that she had spoken to them in their own Cappadocian dialect.

"Come," said the weaver as she led her guests to a small room in the back of the shop. Three small stools bordered a brass tray. It was set with three cups, an open container of highly prized sugar, and some bread and figs that caught Agour's attention immediately.

Beside her was a small stack of kilims she had woven. The beginning rows of a huge tapestry were on her loom. "Welcome," she said, gesturing for them to be seated. Then she poured from the already hot teapot.

Who was she expecting? They wondered as they exchanged glances.

During tea, Agour and Phebe told of Dikuyu and the terrors of Timur. They shared the story of the cisterns, and they all had a good laugh about the boat ride across the Bosporus. The weaver's amber eyes turned to look at Phebe, and the youthful girl felt loved. Agour felt loved too—once he finished off the food.

"Do you have anything to trade? You must need some money for the rest of your journey," she suggested. "A kilim, perhaps?"

Agour and Phebe were more than a little surprised.

How does she know? they both thought, looking at one another in disbelief.

Carefully reaching into her pouch, Phebe sought her brother for approval as she produced the blue kilim with traditional patterns "Yes, of course," she said. "Our family has been weavers for many generations."

"Cappadocia," observed the old woman. "I recognize the colors and style." She turned the kilim over and examined the reverse side, carefully inspecting the tightly woven specimen.

Agour and Phebe were pleased.

"You have another kilim," the old woman said.

Phebe furrowed her brow, wondering what to think.

"Please show me *the* kilim," the weaver implored.

Agour's eyes found Phebe's and held fast. *What does she know?* they thought.

Without breaking her gaze, Phebe reach to the bottom of her bag and grasped *the* kilim at the bottom of her pouch.

She hesitated.

"It is only a small copy," Phebe said, almost swallowing her words as she presented it. "The original is still in Cappadocia." *If it still exists at all*, she thought.

"Yes, I know," replied the old woman, "it is beautiful." Her eyes sparkled as she studied the intricate weaving. The depictions of the ancient scenes seemed to bring satisfaction to her. "The weft is tight. It follows the original Kartun. The red thread is vibrant."

When she had completed her examination, she turned to Phebe and said, "Please stretch out your arm." Phebe cautiously stretched her arm forward while the old woman gently tied a red cord around her wrist. With an affectionate smile, she said. "Wherever you travel, go to the weavers. When they see the red thread, they will help you. I will protect your kilim."

Then she turned to Agour. "You will need your own . . ." Agour extended his hand almost against his own will. After securing the cord around his wrist, she presented him with a small coin bearing the image of the Emperor Justinian. Phebe was sure she recognized it. She felt the outside of her bag for her grandmother's gift. It was the same size but she did not dare to take it out and compare them.

"Farewell," said the weaver, gesturing with her eyes toward the exit of the bazaar.

Agour and Phebe took a few steps, then turned to wave goodbye to the weaver. Nothing was there. Nothing. Not even a shop. Instead, there was just another empty passageway. Agour and Phebe faced each other in disbelief.

What had they just done?

They had surrendered their most precious kilim for two wristbands of crimson and an ancient coin. Alone they faced a new world where they did not even speak the language.

DISCOVER

Present Time

4

SIX CENTURIES LATER

Constantinople / Istanbul

Present Time

"*I*stanbul, or as Mom calls it, Constantinople. We are really here!" exclaimed Phoebe.

The ancient city sparkled in the first rays of morning light.

Derek and Phoebe Paloma held their phones to the window, feverishly snapping pictures and videos. Turkish Airlines flight TK4 from New York banked to the left, giving its VIP passengers a spectacular view. "I can see the shining white dome of the Hagia Sofia," Phoebe said. Phoebe spelled her name the American way, with an o, in order to differentiate her from her maternal grandmother *Phebe*, who spelled it the "old country" way.

"There's the Blue Mosque," Derek said, "and the Sultan's Palace. The old city walls are mostly still standing."

Derek Paloma was sixteen years old, and at six foot two he was nearly as tall as his father. With his sandy hair and blue eyes, he was sure to stand out anywhere. He tried to be inconspicuous by wearing jeans and a plain black T-shirt. He left his designer sneakers back in Phoenix in favor of brown hiking boots.

His sister, Phoebe, was generally unaware of her developing beauty. Her hair was jet black and pulled up into a ponytail. At five feet eight inches, she was tall for her fourteen years. She had also chosen jeans but paired them with a long-sleeved dark green top that brought out the green in her hazel eyes. She had packed dress shoes, and was wearing her blue slip-on sneakers for travel and touring.

"I miss Mom and Philip," Phoebe complained.

In spite of being six thousand miles apart, Derek and Phoebe already felt their mother's touch on their trip. She had chosen their seats, 3A and 3B, to give them the best view of Istanbul. An ear infection prevented seven-year-old Philip and his mother, Helena Paloma, from making the trip.

"Dad, I can't wait to see it," Phoebe exclaimed.

"Today's the day, sweetie!"

"Dad," she protested, "you're not supposed to call me that."

"Sorry."

Dr. Felix Paloma, President of Paloma Gold International, sat behind his kids and smiled approvingly as he watched them drink in the sights.

"Now on final approach. Any news? He texted his team from the air?"

The response was immediate: "Tapestry has become an issue. Rumors could cause delays in the mining operations. —B."

Borodin, head of security for Paloma Gold, greeted the family at the aircraft and led them through back passageways to the VIP lounge. "The paneling on the walls is spruce wood from the forests of Mt. Ararat," he announced before gathering their passports and disappearing in the direction of the customs agents.

On the coffee table was a copy of Istanbul's Hurriet Daily News. Derek read the headline out loud.

"ANCIENT TAPESTRY DISCOVERED BY PALOMA GOLD INTERNATIONAL WHILE MINING NEAR KEYSERI." He handed the paper to his father, who tucked it under his arm.

"Here are your passports," Borodin said, checking each one as he returned it. "Your bags are loaded up and we are good to go. Follow me."

Dr. Paloma was a sizeable man, to say the least. His deep brown eyes constantly surveyed his surroundings. Towering over everybody, except Borodin, he was easy to spot, standing six foot four. His auburn hair waved lightly in the breeze.

Just outside the terminal were three black SUVs and the security team. Their uniforms consisted of black suits, white shirts with open collars, shiny black shoes, and dark sunglasses. "Clear," Derek heard a guard repeat into his microphone.

Born in Istanbul to Russian parents, Igor Borodin stood six foot six and was massive. He knew the city and its ways better than any tour guide and most of all, Borodin was security personified. Every move he made was based on the safety of the ones who had hired him.

"We will drop your bags at the hotel and go see the sights," Borodin declared.

"Where to first?" asked the driver.

"Hagia Sophia," Phoebe called out. "Mom always talked about it."

"Aya Sofia," Dr. Paloma said in Turkish, though it sounded about the same. The driver repeated it into the headsets for the security team, and three black SUVs sped off to one of the world's most unique and celebrated churches.

Borodin loved Istanbul and he loved to share the stories that brought its history to life for his audience. He stopped and faced Hagia Sophia's ancient structure, endeavoring to focus the attention of the Palomas on the majesty they were about to experience.

Suddenly, Dagon, Borodin's second in command, clicked his antiquated flip phone closed. "Excuse me sir." His gravelly voice completely broke the moment. He tapped Dr. Paloma a little too firmly on the shoulder, then gruffly insisted he move out of earshot, which forced everybody to wait.

"It's about the Tapestry and our mining permits." Dr. Paloma apologized when he returned. "I need to get this fixed today, or it will ruin our timing for the rest of our trip," Stay with Borodin. I will go with Dagon, and meet you at the Grand Bazaar this afternoon. Can't forget Mom's carpet, can we?"

"This always happens," Phoebe muttered as she rolled her eyes and watched her dad disappear into the crowd.

"Yeah . . . bye, Dad," Derek groaned.

Borodin drew a deep breath as he turned again to admire the Haya Sofia's massive entrance. "This colossal church has stood watch over Istanbul and Constantinople since AD 537. It was built by the Emperor Justinian."

Derek quickly did the math. "Wow! That means this church has been here for nearly fifteen hundred years," he said.

"It was the largest cathedral in the world for over a thousand years," Borodin said. "About five hundred years ago it became a mosque. Now it is a museum."

He led his guests through Imperial entrance with its nearly thirty-foot-tall doors hanging on decorated bronze frames. The immense hall felt even larger once they were inside. "Some say the dome looks like it is suspended from heaven by a golden chain . . . and I think I agree with them," Borodin stated.

Derek and Phoebe craned their necks to take in the grandeur.

"Is that real gold?" Phoebe asked.

"Yes. It's all real. Real gold. Real silver, copper, and bronze too. Materials were brought from all over the empire. The greenish marble pillars were taken from the pagan Temple of Diana in Ephesus. It was all built by hand," Borodin said. "No machines. No computer designs. It even withstood a 6.7 magnitude earthquake back in 1999, fifteen hundred years after being built. Don't try that in San Francisco."

"Where are the walls covered with mosaics and paintings?" Phoebe asked.

"Yeah," Derek chimed in. "If we miss them, Mom will be . . ." he searched for a word. "Uh, displeased." He grinned.

Borodin went on, "Restoration is underway. Today you can see art that was covered up for centuries. Many beautiful mosaics and frescoes were destroyed over time. Some were destroyed by earthquakes, some by early Christian iconoclasts, and still more by Muslims. It was something like the "cancel culture" of 2020. Fortunately, this is all a museum now. When it was built, it was the biggest building in the world. The great stories of the Bible were all on these walls."

When Phoebe turned around, she was face-to-face with Jesus. Actually, it was the newly restored, one-thousand-year-old mosaic picture of Jesus. Each tiny tile of blue, red, green, and brown had been selected and placed by hand to create the image. Real gold was used in the halo surrounding Jesus' head.

A shiver went up Phoebe's spine. *Did my great-great,* she paused, how many generations she did not know, *grandmother Phebe stand here during her escape from Cappadocia? I wonder what she prayed for?* Phoebe was captivated. Questions flooded her mind. She could not move. It was as if she were frozen in place by the art itself.

After waiting patiently, Borodin gently tapped her arm. "Time to go." She smiled and nodded and wandered off in a daze behind Derek.

It was a short ride to the Sultan's Palace where Borodin continued his tour. "This was the Ottoman Empire version of your White House, Capitol and Pentagon all combined, up until 1918." He led them through a series of ornately tiled rooms lit by elegant stained glass windows. This is the Harem," he said. "This is where the Sultan kept his wives and concubines, not so long ago."

Kept? Concubines? That's slavery. Phoebe thought.

Before she could interrogate him, Borodin shuffled his party through the courts of government and the Sultan's gold private living quarters.

"Grand Bazaar. Established in 1461," Derek read out loud.

"This is where the ancient Silk Road connected Asia to Europe, Marco Polo would have stayed here," Borodin said.

Phoebe spotted her dad standing beneath the sign. "Wow, Dad, I can't believe you got here first. Hagia Sophia was amazing. I couldn't tear myself away. Sorry," she said.

Inside the Grand Bazaar shoppers flooded the maze of small covered streets filled with brightly colored merchandise from all over the world. Giant arched ceilings enclosed the passageways. Voices ricocheted through corridors. Every surface was intricately decorated by generations of artisans. Geometric patterns and paintings of turquoise, red tulips, and deep-blue backgrounds welcomed the visitors.

"For centuries," Borodin called out over the din, "this has been the largest shopping center in the world. Thousands of shops are here. Everything you could want. He picked up piece candy from a sample stand and popped it into his mouth. "Turkish Delight, he said, smacking his lips. You have to try it." The gummy cube topped with white powdered sugar brought mixed reviews from Derek and Phoebe.

"Here we will find textiles, silks, Oriental carpets, jewelry, housewares, clothing, food, and now electronics too." Borodin continued. "Some things here are exceedingly expensive and some are very cheap. Bargaining here is an art form. You have to be a very good shopper to get a good deal. Empires of Hittites, Romans, Byzantines, and Ottomans each left something in the architecture and traditions of our bazaar."

Just then, Derek got a whiff of something grilling. "Let's check it out!" he said. "Just don't lose sight of Dad, that would be trouble."

"Yeah, smells good," she agreed. They followed the scent until they spotted the traditional lamb shawarma rotating on a vertical skewer. Aromas of garlic, saffron, and other exotic spices called to them.

Phoebe tugged her brother's arm, dragging him up to the counter. "Two," she said, holding up two fingers to make sure the clerk understood. Derek presented a five-dollar bill to the young man, who picked up a large knife and pealed the meat off of the vertical spit. He presented them with two pita sandwiches, followed by three small Turkish coins in change.

"Excellent!" Derek mumbled as he bit into the street food with its highly seasoned lamb, lettuce, and yogurt sauce.

Over the din of the bazaar, Phoebe heard Borodin ask her father, "What size carpet." Mrs. Paloma loved shopping as much as her husband hated it. She had expected to pick out a carpet herself. Dr. Paloma rarely showed any nervousness, but he was out of his element shopping for a Turkish carpet to satisfy his wife.

He recounted Helena's words: *"It has to be a carpet from the land of our ancestors. Traditional colors. Reds and turquoise blue, with depiction of stories rather than just geometric patterns. Oh, and preferably with tulips. Have a great time. Just bring back a Turkish carpet for me."*

Borodin led his guests down the corridors and into a popular carpet shop. "Umi, my friend," Borodin said as he greeted the shopkeeper. "This is Dr. Paloma from America."

"How boring is this?" Derek groaned to Phoebe. They wandered away from the shop, but they could still hear their father talking in the distance. I want the highest quality . . . silk, of course."

Derek pointed his sister toward a quiet corridor, and with a grin and a nod they were off. "I'll bet somebody gets a kickback if Dad buys it from Borodin's friend," he said.

"I'm not sure Mom will be happy no matter what he picks," said Phoebe.

As the Paloma kids turned a corner, it got so quiet it felt as if they were wearing noise-cancelling headphones. The 'glitz' was gone in this dark corridor.

"This looks more authentic," Phoebe stated.

"Authentic? There is nothing here. Except that one tiny shop."

"Something special you are looking for?" an old woman asked with broken English.

She wore a white peasant blouse, a blue skirt with a red tulip pattern, and very worn leather sandals. She sat on a low bench in front of a very large loom. *Definitely old world*, Derek thought.

Her shop was filled with the fragrance of lavender incense cancelling out the heavy aroma of garlic from the shawarma. The woman had soft, amber eyes. Her silver hair was mostly concealed by her red, blue, and yellow headscarf.

This must be one of those historical reenactment sites, thought Derek. *The shop looks just like it must have appeared in medieval times.*

"Let's find somebody more interesting," Derek suggested. "Everything in here is really old . . . and so is she."

"Something special you are looking for?" she asked.

"Just a minute." Phoebe held her index finger up to Derek.

She turned and looked directly into the old woman's radiant face and amber eyes.

"What do you mean by *special*?" Phoebe replied.

"Many shops here sell always the same items," the old woman said. "Over and over the same things they make. For my goods, a duplicate you cannot find. Only here you find it," she said, gazing with pride around her rather dingy shop. She obviously saw value where Derek and Phoebe did not.

"Yeah, right. Looks like she hasn't sold anything out of this shop in a hundred years," Derek whispered to Phoebe.

"Look, around her neck."

"Is that Justinian?" Phoebe asked the old woman.

"Yes, they are very rare," the old woman stated, "and very special. I'm surprised you recognized it."

"Our grandmother has one, back in Arizona," Phoebe told her.

The old woman seemed pleased. Dropping her chin and looking over the top of her rimless glasses she asked, "Would you like some tea?" Her smile was infectious and wide, and her eyes sparkled.

"Yes, of course we would," replied Phoebe, without consulting her brother.

Their mother had explained to them before they ever left the States that tea is a custom rarely to be refused. "It is offered to weary travelers and anxious shoppers alike," she often said. "It is much more than a beverage; it is a tradition."

Phoebe and Derek followed her to a small room in the back of her shop. They sat on stools and shared a bit of their story with the old woman.

Softly she leaned forward and said, "I have something you surely must see but cannot buy."

While they sipped their tea, she brought out a small kilim from beneath her stack of ancient goods.

Handing it to Derek, she said, "This one is silk *and* wool. The original is much larger, and very mysterious. In time you will see," she stated. "Unlike many weavings, this tapestry has stories. It was made in the Cappadocia region of Turkey. Have you ever been there?" she asked.

Derek and Phoebe flashed glances at each other. "Our father is taking us there tomorrow," Derek replied with a bit of surprise in his voice.

"Then I want you to have this," she said as she handed the kilim to Derek, who inspected it superficially then passed to Phoebe. The old woman cut a piece of red cord from her spool and tied it around Phoebe's wrist.

"In your travels this cord will increase in meaning to you. It will draw you to people who will help you on your journey . . . and keep you safe."

Turning back to Derek, she insisted, "You will need your own."

"No thank you," he replied, withdrawing his hand as she reached out to him. "No wristbands."

The old woman looked Derek directly in the eye and said, "In time you will understand." A long pause ensued before Derek decided to humor her by extending his arm and allowing her to secure the cord to his wrist.

Satisfaction burst across the old woman's face as if she had made a big sale. "Soon, very soon, you will take a great journey."

"I know, to Cappadocia . . . tomorrow," Phoebe replied, unimpressed.

"Much, much farther," she said. "Farewell, your father will be looking for you, I suppose."

"Goodbye . . . thank you," they said in unison before departing into the quiet alleyway to retrace their steps.

Suddenly, Derek and Phoebe heard yelling in the distance. "That's coming from the bazaar," shouted Derek. "Let's go!" When they rounded a corner, they saw their father surrounded by some angry students.

"That's the guy!" a voice cried out. "I have seen him on television. His company is stealing from us. He is taking artifacts out of the country. Some of them have mystic powers."

Borodin snapped to full alert. "Protect the Boss! Back to the SUVs!" No longer a tour guide, he was now all about security. His team moved into position, forming a phalanx of black suits around Dr. Paloma.

"We have to move . . . now!" Borodin ordered. He slipped the shopkeeper a few Turkish lira for his trouble and simultaneously directed the entourage to return to the entrance.

"Dagon. Get the kids!" Borodin shouted with a motion toward the old passageway where he had watched them wander off. "Find them. Now!"

After just a few steps, Derek and Phoebe were looking into Dagon's angry eyes. "There you are," snapped the exasperated guard. "Let's go!" For a moment he stared at the kilim in Phoebe's hands, then quickly pointed the kids back to the exit and led the way.

Derek and Phoebe tried to keep up with Dagon. They twisted their necks to wave goodbye to the old woman. She was not there. There was no shop. Only a small, dark, time-worn alleyway.

Derek and Phoebe exchanged perplexed glances but had no time to process the event before Dagon's sinister, scratchy voice yelled again. "Hurry up!"

Outside the Grand Bazaar, Dr. Paloma stood beside the SUVs, surrounded by his security detail and the local police. Dagon pushed through the crowd, clearing the way for Derek and Phoebe.

"Sorry," they chorused as they slid into the back seat and stared at the floor, trying to avoid their father's glare.

Borodin gave a signal and the fleet sped off. Derek and Phoebe took one last look at the Grand Bazaar, contemplating their encounter.

"Where did you get this?" asked Dr. Paloma as he gently lifted the kilim from Phoebe's hands.

"From an old woman in a very old shop," Derek replied.

"Well, the joke's on me," said Dr. Paloma. "You found a tapestry after all. Hold this still while I take a picture to send to Mom."

"Hi honey," said the text. "Six thousand miles of travel and this is the only carpet we could get in the Bazaar. I'll try again tomorrow . . . in Cappadocia."

5

ENCOUNTER

Cappadocia

"That was the coolest hotel," Phoebe exclaimed. "My room was a real cave that people lived in long ago."

"Mom picked the hotel," Dr. Paloma said proudly. "Caves, Paloma style. First class all the way."

"What will Mom think of next?"

"Are those the balloons Mom talked about?" Phoebe asked, clapping her hands. "We are going on a balloon ride." They watched the burners of over a hundred multicolored hot air balloons flash on and off, dotting the predawn sky. "Wow, it's almost like Mom is with us. Are we going now?"

"Tomorrow."

"I can't wait, Dad!"

PALOMA GOLD INTERNATIONAL, INC. The sign marked the turnoff from the path of the ancient Silk Road to China.

"I want to get ahead of the story," Dr. Paloma said. "The press thinks I am taking artifacts out of the country and selling them. To make matters worse, there are rumors about some mystical tapestry out there. We want people to see us as the family we are, and that we are preserving Dikuyu for all people."

At the mine, Dr. Paloma and his kids were greeted by local dignitaries and archaeologists. They were also greeted by Salim, who was the head of Paloma Gold's operations in Turkey. A news reporter and photographer were also there, just to document the event.

"Stand here," instructed one of the staffers. "Smile!"

Dr. Paloma struck a fatherly pose between his kids, while his executive team stood behind them.

"Perfect," said the photographer. Then the reporter announced the headline: "Dr. F. Paloma and Family Tour New Discovery in Dikuyu, Cappadocia." The picture would be attached and sent to Istanbul for the *Hürriyet Daily News*.

"Some facts please?" Yusuf began. "How long have you been mining here?"

"Four years," Salim replied. "Last year we discovered this entrance while our miners were removing a vacant stone house. We stopped digging and contacted the government. Now they are managing the excavations," Salim explained. "Follow me. We will go single file until we reach the rooms below. Watch your heads."

"As you know, Dr. Paloma," Salim stated, "this is the largest underground city ever discovered. With our help, sir, seven levels below ground have already been excavated, and there is much more. Experts say the upper levels go back 3,000 years or more. These caves were lived in, off and on, until at least the fourteenth century. They can tell from the artifacts that were found inside."

"Sure is cooler down here," Phoebe observed.

"What about the Tapestry you have discovered?" Yusuf asked. "When will you reveal it?"

"That's just a rumor," Borodin answered. "For centuries there have been stories about a mysterious tapestry. It might be here, but we have not found it. It might be anywhere in this region . . . if it exists at all."

"But we have heard—" Yusuf started to say.

"But nobody has *seen* anything!" Borodin shot back emphatically. "If something is found, you will know."

Borodin could not stop talking about how the underground city had been dug out by hand during the days of the Assyrians and the Hittites.

That's about enough, thought Phoebe.

"Check this out!" Derek whispered, pointing to a passageway to the right. The pair looked to make sure no one was watching.

"Boring-odin will keep Dad occupied," said Phoebe.

Derek pushed past the yellow tape with black stripes and foreign writing on it. They stepped around a large stone wheel sticking out of a slot in the side of the passageway.

"I saw something similar in *Raiders of the Lost Ark*," Derek said. "I think it was some kind of secret door that rolled down to close off the tunnel from invaders."

"Dunno," mumbled Phoebe.

"Can you imagine thousands of people actually living down here? Look at the size of this room," said Derek, awestruck.

Just when their eyes started to adjust, the light from his cell phone started to fade. "I forgot to charge it last night," Derek moaned.

"Me too. I only have a few minutes of battery left," Phoebe complained. She shined her light into the blackness. "It's a little scary."

Derek motioned to Phoebe to turn back. "We had better catch up with Dad."

RrrraaaAAAUUUGGHhh! The sound went right through them like bass notes at a rock concert and didn't stop.

Phoebe and Derek reached for each other as the rumble grew louder and louder.

"Earthquake!" Derek yelled. He grabbed Phoebe and dropped to the ground, tucking her under him and trying to protect her.

The earth raged. The ground heaved under them. Falling rocks ricocheted against their hard hats. The pair tried to cover their noses and mouths, but the dust still made it impossible to breathe. Then again, they could hardly breathe for fear itself.

Eventually the shaking stopped.

"Khaauggh! Khaauugh!" Phoebe tried to cough out the dust.

The room echoed back, "Khaauugh." The sound was suspended in the dust-filled darkness. Derek and Phoebe clung to each other. It was cold and black and silent as a tomb.

"Are we dead?" Phoebe sputtered.

"We will be fine," Derek whispered. He wasn't really sure of anything except trying not to scare his sister.

Phoebe and her brother tried to clear their eyes, remove the dust from their teeth, and resume breathing. Despite all the banter of brother-sister love and sarcasm, they had never held on to each other so tightly. Shivers ran through their bones.

Gradually they began to ease their grips without completely letting go. *Was this it? Would anybody ever find them? Were they already dead?*

"Phoebe," Derek said, squeezing her hand, "we will get out of this."

Silence.

"Do you see that?" Derek whispered.

Their eyes strained into the emptiness where a tiny speck of blue light was trying to overcome the profound blackness. Derek tried his cell phone again but without success. Phoebe held Derek's hand tightly as they watched the light grow slightly brighter.

"It's coming toward us," Phoebe whispered.

Their hearts pounded. To run in the darkness was not an option. Their muscles tensed to face whatever it was. Finally, the light came close enough that they could make out the figure of a man. His steps were slow and deliberate.

"Get up," Derek whispered. Phoebe did not move.

"Get up," Derek repeated. "If we can stand up, we are not dead."

Well, that would be a relief, Phoebe thought. She grabbed Derek and they lifted each other to their feet.

The approaching form was tall, wiry, and bent like an old man. He wore a long shadowy robe and was almost as tall as Derek. In his hand he held a staff that extended above his head and curved back around like a shepherd's crook. At its apex was a jewel that emitted a bluish light. His face was obscured by the broad brim of his hat and the fluffy white beard that surrounded his face.

He stopped.

"No dust," Derek whispered to Phoebe.

"What do you mean?"

"Everything here is covered with earthquake dust . . . except him," he said.

"Don't be afraid," a baritone voice spoke slowly.

"Yeah, good idea," Phoebe said to herself. She could almost hear her knees knocking together.

"I am Yaldar," said the voice.

"Of course you are," Phoebe shot back. "And I'm Wonder Woman. Our dad is back there somewhere, and he's freaking out.

He *will* find us. I know he is just on the other side of that stupid millstone. Do you know how to get us out of here?"

"Yes," Yaldar replied in a measured tone that should have calmed Phoebe. It wasn't working.

"Then let's go," she commanded. "We need to get to our dad."

"All in good time," Yaldar stated.

"Good time?" Phoebe pressed him. "How about *now*? Now would be a *very* good time!"

Yaldar waited for her to settle down, but she didn't. "Don't be afraid," he repeated. This time Phoebe calmed down just a little. She decided to listen, if only to get time to prepare her next salvo.

"The stone door has closed and cannot be rolled open," Yaldar explained. "It was designed by the ancients to protect them from invasion."

"Great!" she said. "In a couple of minutes our dad will push the stone away and we will get out of here."

"It's not that easy. The stone is like the one that closed off the grave of Jesus. Easy to close. One person can roll it *down* the slope. But it takes many people, tools and some special wisdom to roll it back up."

Derek took Phoebe's hand in an effort to calm her. "So, you're saying we're trapped? And you can't help us?" she said.

"No," Yaldar replied. "I can help you." He turned to Derek. "How's your leg?"

Until that moment Derek had not realized that his leg was hurting. Now the pain was screaming at him. He reached down to feel the trickle of warm fluid on his ankle.

How did he know?

"During the earthquake a very important clay jar broke," Yaldar said. "Evidently you were cut by a flying piece of pottery."

Huh? Wondered Derek. *You know all of that in the dark?*

The blue light at the top of Yaldar's staff brightened, revealing his slight smile. Phoebe and Derek could see his weathered face and white beard. There was not enough light to discern the color of the eyes that framed his imposing nose.

Derek turned to check the way they had come. By the dim light of Yaldar's staff, he could see that there was no way to move the millstone that blocked their escape. He felt hopeless, but he wasn't giving up.

"Check out that broken jar," Yaldar said, pointing to the pottery.

"The bottom part is still intact and holding some kind of fabric," Derek said. "Pieces are scattered around on the ground. Something is still wound up in the jar. It is impossible to tell anything without more light."

"It is called the Tapestry of Time," Yaldar said. "It has been in that jar since the Mongol invasion over six hundred years ago."

"Big deal," Derek said, shrugging. "What's in a tapestry anyway? Isn't it just a rug?"

"Ah, funny you should ask," Yaldar responded. "There's a whole lot more here than just a rug. Think about it this way: what if you want to share a story with the people who live after you, but they cannot read? What should you do?"

"Draw pictures on the cave wall, I guess?" Derek proposed.

"And what if you wanted to take the story with you?"

"Huh?" responded Derek, confused.

"Make a tapestry with pictures in it?" Phoebe blurted. "Then you could roll it up and take it with you."

"Exactly," Yaldar replied. "And that is precisely what we have here. Stories that teach us. Stories that connect us to God. And even some stories that reveal the future. Each story has been woven separately. It took almost fifteen centuries before all of the pieces could be gathered and assembled into one tapestry."

"So," Derek said, "you're telling us that the rolled up rug is some kind of special relic?"

Yaldar nodded slowly.

"Does it have powers or something?"

"That is for you to discover," said Yaldar. "Some believe that once upon a time it protected the inhabitants of Dikuyu from the Mongols."

The Tapestry? Phoebe turned to Derek, feeling a chill.

"Remember the story Grandma Phebes used to tell us about how Mom's family came to America? It was always so cool to hear the story how they left a tapestry behind."

Yaldar remained silent for a while before he said, "Well, you are just in time."

Just then, the aftershock hit.

❋ ❋ ❋

Phoebe and Derek clung together as dust drifted from the ceiling. Yaldar held onto his staff and swayed like he was riding a subway.

Yaldar said, "There is someone you need to meet who will help you understand. I will take you now." The glow of Yaldar's staff lit only the next stride or two into an otherwise black abyss. After a few terrifying steps, the trio came face-to-face with a solid cave wall.

"I thought he knew where to go," Phoebe whispered to Derek.

Yaldar stood very erect and softly tapped his staff to the floor of the cave. He waited. A small red dot finally appeared on the cave wall in front of the trio. As it grew, it became an oval, taller than it was wide yet exactly tall enough to accommodate Yaldar and Derek. The perimeter wobbled and glowed. Now it was more purple than red.

6

THE WEAVER

Workshop Beyond Time

Through the portal Phoebe saw a large room with smooth walls lighted by flickering candles and oil lamps set into niches.

"This way," Yaldar directed. He lowered his head so that his hat cleared the portal and stepped through. Then he extended his hand back to Phoebe.

Phoebe did not move. *What are our choices?* she wondered. *We can follow this guy and face whatever is over there, or we can stand here in the dark again.* Phoebe looked at Derek, then back to Yaldar. She stepped through the portal, but she did not take his hand. *That would be too much,* she reasoned.

After clearing the portal, Derek watched the glowing band shrink to a red dot and fade away.

By the light of the oil lamps, the kids could finally see Yaldar more clearly. His eyes were light brown. His cheeks were high, and his white beard framed a gentle smile. His long, off-white robe was gathered at his waist by a braided rope belt. The index finger of his left hand bore a gold ring with a shiny red stone of some kind. *A ruby or garnet,* thought Derek.

And then there was the hat. When the brim flopped forward

it was almost impossible to see Yaldar's face. What the brim did not hide was concealed by his beard. That left his nose that was, as Phoebe thought, more than ample and less than straight.

Yaldar's staff also was far more visible now. The grain of the wood appeared to be in motion. In the lighted room the bluish-green stone glowed more softly.

He's not that scary after all, thought Phoebe.

Yaldar grinned and tipped his head as he led the travelers into a larger room with even more oil lamps and candles. On one side of the room, an old woman sat before a large weaver's loom on a low bench.

"I thought you would have been here sooner," she said without looking up. The woman's voice seemed vaguely familiar. It was so gentle and welcoming that Derek and Phoebe began to let their guard down . . . just a little.

"The tea is getting cold," she commented as she rose to greet her visitors.

Is she expecting us? Phoebe wondered.

Yaldar made the introduction. "Derek and Phoebe, may I present to you The Weaver, Sophia."

"That's my cousin's name," Phoebe said delightedly. "It means *wisdom*."

Derek started to say, "We have met," but he wasn't sure. He turned to Phoebe and raised an eyebrow to ask a silent question. After all, they had only met one weaver, and that was back in Istanbul.

"Look at her eyes," Phoebe whispered. "It has to be . . . but how could she get here?"

"I am Sophia," she said. "Welcome to my workshop." She approached the kids and looked them up and down like a grandma checking out her grandkids. She led them to a round, hammered brass tray on a low stand surrounded by four low stools. On the tray were four glasses for tea, containers with sugar and milk, and a few cookies. Everything was arranged exactly as it had been in the Grand Bazaar.

Derek and Phoebe glanced at each other but said nothing.

"Thank you for coming," Sophia said as she poured the tea.

Yeah. We had lots of options and we chose this, thought Phoebe. Then she sat down, extended her hands, and received the tea.

Sophia watched Derek wince and check his leg as he took his seat. "It's nothing," he shrugged, wiping his hands on his jeans.

"Not really nothing," she replied as she left the room and returned with a small cloth bandage, which she secured using a thin red cord. Then she rose to her feet. "Come with me," she said, leading them to a large worktable nearby. "Do you recognize it?" There was a pile of weavings and a broken clay jar on the table.

"I . . . I think so," Phoebe responded. "From the earthquake?"

"Yes," Sophia answered. "You saw it in the cave. It's in bad shape, I'm sorry to say. For centuries this Tapestry hung on the wall over there." She pointed to a niche. "Now it must be restored and revealed to the world, and this is my workshop where we will do it."

"O-o-kay?" stammered Derek. "What makes it so special?

"Like any tapestry, pictures are woven together to tell a story," Sophia began. "Often it is about the triumph of a great warrior, or the glories of a great ruler. For a tapestry, the best artisans are always sought out. A sketch that weavers call a *kartun* is created. The materials are all coordinated, and the sequence of the story panels are established. Each weaver creates his part. The master weaver then supervises the weaving and final assembly according to the design in the kartun. When it is finished, any observer can see the story.

"Okay, this Tapestry tells stories. Why is it so different from other Tapestries?" Derek asked.

Sophia continued. "Unlike other tapestries, the pictures in

the Tapestry of Time were woven at various times over centuries by artisans from all over the world. It is made of linen, wool, silk, and a little goat and camel hair. You would think it impossible for the story of a great ruler to be told through these diverse pieces that are faded and separated. But once we restore it, you will see."

"Great," Phoebe said. "Our dad loves this kind of thing. He would love to donate it to the museum, or whatever you want, and probably pay for the restoration."

"In order to restore the Tapestry, I need special materials," the weaver said.

"Look," Phoebe reacted. "This tapestry thing is very cool and all, but we just want to get back to our dad. Can you help us or not?"

"Yes, I can help you, but only if you help me."

"Sure. What do you need?" asked Derek.

"Cords and threads stained by blood," Sophia answered.

"That's pretty heavy. Where do you get that?" he questioned.

"Yaldar will take you. There will be forces and people that do not want you to succeed. He will help you."

Just then Phoebe's mind went to the kilim in the old frame hanging by the fireplace at home. *What does that have to do with all of this?* Phoebe wondered.

"And what if we refuse to go?" she challenged.

"Then somebody else will be found, for there is no doubt that the Tapestry will be restored and revealed. But I have no plan B," Yaldar said.

Derek and Phoebe turned away from Yaldar and the weaver and consulted with each other to make their decision.

We are in a cave with no visible way out. We have no Plan B either. They knew what their dad would say at a time like this.

"Let's roll," they declared in unison.

MISSION

7

EDEN

The Beginning of Humanity

*Y*aldar tapped the floor gently with his staff. Again, the red dot appeared on the wall before them. It wobbled and pulsed as before, straining to accommodate Derek's height and Yaldar's hat. Once it took on its oval shape and reached its full proportion, the center opened up like a lens on a camera, revealing a cave on the other side.

Yaldar stepped through first. Derek checked his surroundings and followed.

Phoebe hesitated. She was pretty angry, but when she stepped through the portal her anger evaporated. She was overcome by a state of peace and a sense of joy . . . even ecstasy.

"Your quest begins now," Yaldar announced. "We will visit many places shown in the Tapestry. In order for the weaver to restore each scene, you will need to bring back something from each event with a blood-red color, preferably bloodstained."

"Watch your step," Yaldar cautioned as he left the cave and disappeared into a thick fog.

"I can barely see the ground," Derek commented.

"Look at your clothes!" Phoebe exclaimed. "That's the lightest camo-like fabric I have ever seen. I can hardly see you. You look like the fog itself. My clothes are the same!" She rubbed the soft texture between her thumb and forefinger.

Very cool, thought Derek.

"My shoes are gone. I guess we don't need them here. It really feels good just to go barefoot," Phoebe said. "Smell the flowers? It is overwhelming. Like orange and lemon blossoms mixed with so many wonderful floral scents. It is beyond any perfume."

As the fog lifted, the vast, lush garden came into view. Yaldar ducked to avoid a giant clump of grapes. He broke off a sprig and handed some to Derek and some to Phoebe. "Watch out for the seeds," he quipped. "It'll be thousands of years before the seedless kind are cultivated."

A riot of sounds echoed around them. Giant birds were suspended in the sky by the slightest breeze. Brightly colored birds flitted from trees and hummingbirds from flower to flower. In the canopy monkeys glided through the treetops.

"Over there I see huge herds of grazing animals. Too many to count," Phoebe exclaimed. "And the wind in the trees resonates like low flutes."

"This is another world," breathed Derek.

Yes . . . it is," said Yaldar.

"Lush doesn't come close to describing it," Phoebe added.

"Look," said Derek, pointing to the wide river that flowed through the middle of the Garden. "This is the clearest water I have ever seen. Can we drink here, Yaldar?"

"Of course. Drink up. You could even fill your water bottles, if you had them."

Derek crouched and scooped the cool water into his hands. "I am so thirsty. My throat is still dry from all that cave dust."

Just then a tiger strolled up to the opposite bank of the river.

"A saber-tooth," Phoebe whispered.

It glanced at the kids and Yaldar as if to say hello, then began to drink.

There was no fear.

"Whoa," said Derek. "I can't believe that just happened."

"Then check this out," said Yaldar.

From behind them the ground began to rumble. The bushes danced. Suddenly the neck of a giant brontosaurus extended over their heads and bent down to the water. It looked at the tiger. It turned its giant brown eyes to observe the kids. Then it drank. Gallons of water rumbled through the beast's monstrous neck.

Derek and Phoebe stood mesmerized as they watched the tiger and the dinosaur drink their fill and walk away casually.

"Can we swim in it?" Derek asked.

"If we had time," chuckled Yaldar, "But remember, we are on a mission. Time has us."

"It is soooo peaceful here," sighed Phoebe. Her mind flashed back to a moment when she was sitting on the porch with her granddad back in Indiana. *But without bugs*, she thought.

"Life as it is supposed to be," mumbled Derek.

"Precisely," Yaldar agreed.

"Are we in heaven?" Phoebe asked. "This is so perfect."

"Not even close." Yaldar winked. "Guess again."

"I never imagined dinosaurs in heaven. Are we are in the past?" Derek asked. "Maybe we are in some ancient time."

"Ooh, wait. Is this the Garden of Eden?" Phoebe asked. "Are Adam and Eve here somewhere?"

"Yes. And everything is just about to change," Yaldar replied.

Derek recalled the story. "Adam and Eve weren't supposed to eat the apple, were they?"

"But they did," said Phoebe, "and God got angry and cursed them and sent them out of the Garden. And He cursed the snake too."

"Well, not exactly," Yaldar replied. "Let's check it out."

Yaldar led the pair along a winding path beside the river. Their heads whirled as they tried to take it all in. Brightly colored birds dotted the sky. Frolicking about were animals they recognized, and some they had never imagined.

"It is so vast," Phoebe exclaimed. "And the breeze feels like a caress."

Two trees towered high above the rest of the canopy. They were visible for miles in every direction. The first one they came to had plump fruits of gold, green, and yellow weighing its branches, while its bright leaves glistened. "That is the Tree of Life," Yaldar stated.

"Have Adam and Eve eaten from this tree?" Derek asked.

"Up to now, yes," replied Yaldar.

"So where is the *other* tree?" Derek asked.

"Not far," Yaldar said. He led them over a hill.

Phoebe drew a breath and held it when the tree came into view. "Stunning," she declared. "It is as tall as the Tree of Life. The branches look like they are weeping under the weight of all the bright red fruit."

"This is The Tree of the Knowledge of Good and Evil," Yaldar stated.

Beyond beautiful!" Derek exclaimed.

Its leaves shone a deep green and shadowed a monstrous trunk. Its branches were bent low by the weight of enticing red fruit.

When they drew closer, Derek and Phoebe found a vantage point behind a banyan tree. "Those aren't exactly apples, are they?" Phoebe observed. "They are bigger and even redder."

"I can see two people standing at the opposite edge of the clearing. I'm guessing that is Adam and Eve," Derek chuckled.

Phoebe started to say something witty like, "Good guess, Sherlock," but instead she blurted, "We need to stop them!"

She started to jump into action, but immediately Yaldar tilted his staff and blocked her. He lifted his finger to his lips to indicate silence. They overheard the conversation.

"I know what Elohim* told you," they heard Eve say to Adam. "But the serpent assured me we wouldn't die. We would just see the world the way Elohim sees it. Oh, Adam, that is what I want. Don't you? To be just like Elohim? What could be wrong with that?"

Eve held the ripe, red fruit for a few moments, just looking and waiting for Adam to respond. Her face changed. She was mesmerized. She wanted it. In an instant her bright, white teeth penetrated its radiant skin. Derek and Phoebe's eyes widened as the juicy seeds of the blood-red fruit splattered onto Eve's skin and drizzled down her naked body.

"Look," Derek said. "She is getting some kind of rush. She is blushing and waving her hands in front of her. And look at her eyes; they are huge."

"Oh, Adam," they heard her say. "I can't describe this feeling. I'm not dead! I never felt so alive to new feelings. You have to try this."

Phoebe and Derek held their breath as the half-eaten trophy fruit passed from Eve's hand to Adam's.

They watched in horror as Adam took his notorious.

"He's getting a rush too," Phoebe said. "They are liking it!"

Adam dropped the fruit. The blood-red orb minus their bites now lay at the feet of Elohim's highest creation—humanity. Speechless, Derek and Phoebe watched.

"Did you feel that?" asked Phoebe. "A cold wind is kicking up from out of somewhere." The trees started to groan, the pools of water began to roil, and the sky seemed to swirl and darken.

"Adam?" came the voice.

"It is Elohim! He is going to be mad at us," Eve whispered. "We will die, won't we?"

"I'm sure of it," Adam said.

"The serpent told me we wouldn't die, but now I'm certain he lied to me," cried Eve. "Everything feels different. My skin feels weird. My stomach is churning. Look, my hands are shaking."

"Why did you do this?" Adam demanded. He turned to Eve and started to raise his voice. His face reddened. His eyes flashed with anger. "I can't believe this. The fruit was beautiful. The rush we got was awesome. What . . . went . . . wrong?"

Eve tried to draw close to Adam.

"Leave me alone," he snapped. "Don't touch me! Nothing feels right."

"I know," Eve said, recoiling. "I have sensations I can't describe. They are awful. I feel exposed."

"Adam?" The voice was closer.

"Shh . . . He's here," whispered Eve.

"I feel it too," Phoebe said, instinctively crouched down. They stood just barely within earshot.

"I-I'm af-fraid of H-Him," Adam stuttered.

"Will He kill us?" Eve questioned.

"Hide," Adam whispered as he pulled Eve into the bushes.

Derek and Phoebe felt compelled to hide, too, although they had no idea why. Yaldar followed them and made sure they kept their distance. Gone was the amazing fragrance of the bushes where they were hiding. Even the wind felt so cold and different. Not a caress, but a harbinger.

"We are going to die," Eve said, still shaking. "I'm so afraid."

"Adam? Eve? Where are you?" The voice sounded more like the voice of a parent separated from a wandering child.

"Are you hiding? What are you afraid of?"

"Death," whispered Eve. "I can't even breathe."

"He knows we are here," Adam said. "We *have* to face Him."

When Adam and Eve finally stepped back into the clearing, the fruit was still lying on the ground, a sober witness to their disobedience. They emerged wearing leafy cover-ups that they had quickly tied around themselves.

Elohim stopped at the far end of the clearing where Derek and Phoebe could not see Him. He was clothed in shimmering light so intense there was no way to discern His features. He moved without walking and spoke without talking, yet they heard Him clearly. The light of His presence flooded the open space around Adam and Eve.

What are those leaves all about?" Elohim asked as He stood gazing at them. "You look silly."

"We did it because the wind was cold . . . and we were naked," Adam replied.

"Why was the wind cold? And who told you that you were naked?"

Adam and Eve stared at the ground.

"Did you eat of the fruit of *the* tree?"

"Yes . . ." Adam's voice trailed off.

Then he added. "The woman that you gave me, gave it to me, and I ate it."

"Boy is that lame," sputtered Phoebe. "He is not only blaming Eve, he's blaming God for giving Eve to him. Gross!"

Derek struggled to find a response but gave up.

"Everything is different now," they heard Eve say. "Even the animals are not acting the same."

"Is this where they are cursed by Elohim?" Derek asked Yaldar.

"Pay close attention," Yaldar answered. "There is much more to the story."

"Are we going to die?" Adam asked Elohim sheepishly.

"Today there will be death," Elohim replied, "but it will not be you."

Derek turned to Yaldar and asked, "What about the curse?"

Suddenly, rustling through the leaves was a snake-like shadow slithering with pride for the deception he had brought to humanity. His tongue darted to and fro from between his long white fangs, as if to mock God. Elohim cursed the serpent. Then He cursed the ground, so that it became hard work for Adam to hunt and grow food.

But He did not curse Adam or Eve.

"Consequences are not curses," Yaldar said. "There is even a blessing. Listen!"

"Eve," Elohim began, "your descendants will always contend with the serpent. Eventually, in the future, one of your descendants will crush its head."

With that, Elohim drew a shining sword out of nowhere. He lifted a small goat by its hind legs, and with a single flash of the scimitar, He slit the throat of the unsuspecting sacrifice.

Blood splattered everywhere. It splattered onto Adam. It splattered onto Eve. The animal's innocent lifeblood drained onto the ground beside the fallen fruit.

Phoebe started to scream. It was a "silent scream" for the ages. She stared in horror at the spectacle. Her mouth and eyes were wide open but did not emit a sound.

"Whhaaa?" She tried to scream again. "Blood is everywhere."

She raised her arm to block a droplet flying toward her. It was intercepted by the red strand the weaver had tied to her wrist. Immediately, the strand began pulsating with iridescent red light.

"It all happened so fast," exclaimed Derek. "I saw His back, then the flash of His sword."

The shining light of Elohim settled softly in the Garden, still holding the bloody animal. Elohim skinned the goat and from the skins made leather garments for each of them.

"This will protect you from the winds to come, but you can no longer stay here. You must go now." He gestured to a path heading eastward.

"Are we going to die?" Eve asked.

"You will die . . . in time," Elohim said. "Today, guilt and the sentence of death have entered the world, but only this innocent animal has died as a sacrifice for you. Your clothing will remind you of what happened here."

"Look at your wrist," Yaldar said to Phoebe. "The strand on your wrist is glowing with the color we need to begin restoring the Tapestry. That is our mission."

Before they could consider the moment, a chilled wind whipped through the Garden, stripping leaves from the trees and stirring up dust.

"This way," Yaldar shouted over the gathering windstorm. He pointed to a cliff that was barely visible in the west.

"Didn't Adam and Eve go the other way?" Derek asked.

"Yes, and two huge cherub-angels will guard the entrance to the Garden so they cannot come back," Yaldar explained. "Our portal will also close soon."

"Yaldar, I'm freezing," Phoebe cried out over the raging of the wind. "How much farther? This thin clothing is worthless."

"Not far," he said, and quickly found the route back to the cave.

With the morning fog long gone, they could now see a narrow path along the edge of a sheer cliff. The drop-off was terrifying.

"Did we come down this way?" Derek asked.

"Yes."

"I should have been scared to death."

"There was no death when we entered the Garden. Better watch your steps now," Yaldar warned.

Once inside the cave, Yaldar tapped his staff to the floor. The rosy laser dot appeared on the back wall, and the travelers watched the portal take shape with its wobbly, bright red oval perimeter. When it reached its full size, it opened, inviting them to cross over.

RESTORATION BEGINS

Workshop

Sophia was waiting. Her smile and warm eyes welcomed the weary travelers. Still shaking from the cold, Phoebe was thankful her clothing had changed back to a much warmer peasant style.

"Tea?" Sophia asked.

Derek nodded. He was hoping for more than just tea when he took a stool and sat down.

Phoebe warmed her hands with the hot cup.

Sophia spotted the red band on Phoebe's wrist. Sheer ecstasy burst across her face. "May I see," she asked gently, reaching out to examine it.

The red fiber responded to the weaver's touch. It released itself into her fingers as if it was a lost child returning to its mother.

"Come, the loom and the Tapestry are waiting for us," she said. They followed her to her workshop, where she sat down on her low bench and lifted the loom's shuttle.

"It was you in the bazaar in Istanbul, wasn't it?" asked Phoebe.

Sophia nodded and smiled. "I am so glad you are here."

"Usually the shuttle is very quick," Sophia commented. "But today it wants to embrace the crimson thread." Gently she fed the red strand into the Tapestry. With each inch, the Tapestry's images of the Garden of Eden brightened.

There were the images of Adam and Eve standing together. The fruit and the sacrifice lay side by side at their feet. It was all there. The red color appeared first. Gradually, the greens, yellows, and subtle blues filled themselves in.

It felt like an instant replay for Derek and Phoebe.

"What else did you see, my dear?" asked Sophia.

"The part about knowing good and evil," Phoebe answered.

"Before they knew good and evil, what did they know?" Sophia asked.

Phoebe pondered the question. "Only good, Phoebe replied. She sounded surprise by her discovery.

"So, what did they really gain?" the weaver posed.

"The knowledge of evil. That is not a win, is it?" Phoebe answered.

"I think there is something more to it," Derek suggested. "It isn't just the knowledge of evil, but the knowledge of the difference, right? Animals never stop and say, 'that's wrong,' they just follow their instinct, kill, and eat without any reasoning."

Sophia looked at them with a satisfied smile. "Yes. There are people like that." She led them back to her table. "Please sit down. You must eat and rest before your next journey." She disappeared into the recesses of the cave and returned with some dates, hummus, pita bread, and cheese.

"I was hoping for In-N-Out," Derek quipped to Phoebe as he loaded up a pita and attacked it like a starving tiger.

9

MORIAH

c. 2000 BC

"Now can we go get our dad?" Phoebe asked.

Yaldar tilted his head and gave her an understanding look. "Much remains to do, but you see how it works now. Before long, you will begin to see the whole Tapestry come together."

Sophia gently tied a new strand on Phoebe's wrist and patted her hand.

Yaldar again turned and stared into the blackness of the cave and tapped his staff to the floor. This time they could see all the way to the back wall where the small red dot began to grow.

As they moved toward the portal, Derek jumped in front of Yaldar and faced him directly. "Look, Mr. Yaldar. Don't play games with us. We want to know *exactly* where you are taking us. It feels like we are getting farther from our dad."

"We've covered this," Yaldar replied softly. "The fastest way to get to your dad requires the restoration of the Tapestry. You saw it. You saw what happened when the blood-soaked thread touched the tapestry. We need to keep moving."

The tiny red dot appeared on the cave wall and slowly expanded into its luminescent oval band. It wobbled as before and took on a primordial deep purple glow again, sizing up Derek and Yaldar for height.

Yaldar stepped through and extended his hand back to Phoebe. She hesitated, then reluctantly took his hand. Derek followed.

When the portal closed behind them, they were in a cave nearly thirty feet square. At its apex it was about ten feet high.

"Limestone," Derek commented. "Remember how Dad always used to test us on rock types?"

The kids followed Yardar as they climbed onto a large boulder that sat above the cave entrance. "This is the Foundation Stone," he said. "One day King Solomon will build the Temple right here on this mountain. Across that valley to the east is the Mount of Olives, and beyond it the Jordan River. Remember this place."

The travelers followed Yaldar down a worn gravel path and into an olive grove. Yaldar sat down on a large rock under the shade of ancient, gnarled olive trees. Then he patted the rock for the kids to sit beside him and gazed up the trail they had just descended. It was a peaceful day. The desert air blew softly on their faces. They waited.

Eventually an old man came riding from the south. He sat on a donkey and was accompanied by three young men who walked beside him.

The old man's long white beard shone in the sunlight, especially in contrast to his black desert robe and turban.

"Abraham is known by believers as the father of faith," Yaldar said.

When they came close enough, Yaldar called out, "Peace," and rose to his feet. Derek and Phoebe followed his lead. "Peace," they said.

In his eyes was a far-off gaze. His battered walking stick may once have looked as nice as Yaldar's, but no longer. "It has been many years," Abraham said as he greeted Yaldar. "This is my son Isaac and our two servants. We are here at Moriah to sacrifice to Elohim."

"He sure took his time getting off of the donkey," Phoebe commented as he lowered himself onto the rock next to Yaldar.

Isaac sent his servants to water the donkey at the Kidron brook. Then he turned to Derek and Phoebe. "That's my dad. He was a hundred when I was born. I am Isaac," he introduced himself.

"I am Phoebe."

"I am Derek."

Derek did the math. *If Isaac is about the same age as me, Abraham must be one hundred sixteen or so*, he guessed, sneaking another glance.

"And I thought Yaldar was old," said Phoebe.

Isaac seemed to be relieved to have somebody to talk to. He led Derek and Phoebe to a shady spot deep in the olive grove and away from his father. He was a little shorter than Derek, very wiry and keenly aware of his surroundings. A small gecko distracted him when it darted under a rock, then he turned back to Derek.

"Look, my dad is the best dad anyone could ask for. But I'm afraid he is losing something, if you know what I mean." Isaac rolled his eyes.

"What if God doesn't *provide* like Dad said?" The young man stared at the ground as he continued. "Three days ago, we left our home to come here and make a sacrifice on Mt. Moriah. Dad is always well prepared, especially when it comes to worshipping Elohim. He split the wood at home and carried it on the donkey for three days. As if there's no wood here to burn?" He pointed with his eyes to the olive grove. "He brings his own kindling wood and keeps it very dry. He even practiced starting a fire by making sparks with a flint. He sharpens his knife in order to slaughter the sacrifice, but . . ." his voice trailed off as he looked up at the hill.

"So, what is different this time?" Phoebe whispered.

Tension strained Isaac's voice as he said, "Look around. Do you see a lamb, or a goat, or . . . anything to sacrifice?"

Derek and Phoebe dutifully looked around and, of course, saw no such animal.

"See?" Isaac continued. "The way my dad has been, I'm starting to think that the sacrifice is going to be me."

"You? No way!" Phoebe exclaimed. "Did you ask him?"

"Not directly, Isaac replied. "He's acting funny. But this is not my first camping trip. Dad has always taken me with him before when he went to make sacrifices to Elohim. Around the fires at night, he always loved to tell me the story how Elohim came to him when he was ninety-nine years old. He and mom had given up on ever having a child. He told me how Elohim promised him that he would have a son by the next year. That's when I was born. 'You are the child of God's promise,' he would always say. 'The Lord will make us a blessing to the entire earth.' What's more, I'm his only son. I had a half-brother, but he went to the desert, so I'm the only heir. Think about it. What would happen to the promise if I die?"

"So what did he say when you asked him about the lamb?" Derek asked.

"Jehovah Jireh," he said. "That means 'God will provide.' "

"That's it?" Derek questioned. "No explanation? It does sound a little weird. How can we sacrifice *to* God, if the sacrifice is provided *by* God anyway?"

"It's worse than that," Isaac said, shaking his head. "The pagans around here sacrifice their children to the gods. For a moment I wondered. But that's not Elohim's way. If I die, the promise dies. Can't you see? It's really *my* promise as much as his now."

Derek wanted to say something to ease his fear. "What are you going to do?" he asked.

"Go with Dad," replied Isaac.

"Where?" Phoebe asked.

Isaac flashed a glance up the hillside toward the Foundation Stone. "We will build an altar, and we will sacrifice to Elohim."

"Even if it's you?" Derek asked in astonishment.

"I don't really have to decide until I get there," Isaac whispered.

Nobody seemed to know what to say after that, so they just sat, looking up at the mountainside, until they felt a breeze. It stirred Abraham into action. He stood up, looked at Isaac, pointed to the wood, and said, "Load up."

"It doesn't make sense," Isaac continued, trying to sort out his predicament. "If I am sacrificed, the promise would become a lie."

"No way," Phoebe blurted. She caught herself, dropped her head, and stared at the ground.

Isaac turned to Derek. "Can you give me a hand with this?"

Derek and Isaac, together with the servants, took the ropes off of the donkey and strapped the bundle of wood to Isaac's back.

"Where did you learn to tie a knot like that?" Abraham asked.

Oops, Derek thought. *Can't tell him about the mountaineering camp in Colorado.* "My uncle." Derek felt the twinge of guilt as the lie spurted past his lips. He looked down and checked the knot again.

Abraham turned to the servants. "Wait here. Take care of the donkey," he commanded them. "The lad and I will go up the mountain and worship, then we will come back together."

"Goodbye," Isaac said to Phoebe and Derek with a note of finality.

Suddenly the weight of the wood shifted, throwing Isaac off balance.

"Help him!" Before the words were out of Phoebe's mouth, Derek had caught the wood. He steadied Isaac for a few steps and offered to carry it.

"No," Isaac insisted. "I have to carry this myself."

The travelers watched Isaac strain under the weight of the wood as he walked with his father up the path toward the top of the mountain.

"Quick!" Yaldar motioned for the kids to follow him. They kept out of sight, hiking up the mountainside, until they finally found a hiding place behind some brambles where they could see the rock altar.

Abraham was moving slower with every step. When they finally reached the Foundation Stone, he directed Isaac to take the bundle from his shoulders and arrange the wood on the rock altar.

Isaac faced his father.

Abraham's tired eyes looked to the sky. *Did you give Isaac to me just to take him away again and break an old man's heart after all of these years? I will make this offering. And I still believe you will keep your promise*, he prayed.

Isaac stepped back. "Father," he said, "I don't have to go along with this. I can run. I can still have a life. You are asking me to believe that you really heard God and that we will go back down this mountain together!"

"Yes," Abraham affirmed.

"I can't believe it. Isaac's getting on the altar himself," Phoebe whispered. "Obviously, there's no way any hundred-twenty-year-old man could possibly force him to do this."

"If what Abraham believes is not true, then this will be the last thing Isaac ever does," Derek whispered back. "I wouldn't put up with it. Besides, Dad would never ask me to do anything like this."

"Elohim is weaving a picture for us," Yaldar said. "Watch."

Abraham bound his only son to the altar.

Phoebe's heart pounded as they watched in horror. Abraham lifted the knife high into the air and held it. Slowly, he turned his head and looked away from his son. Now Derek and Phoebe could see the anguish on Abraham's face. His muscles tensed and his knife began to shake.

"Abraham . . ." A voice pierced the sky.

"AB-RA-HAM!"

Phoebe and Derek almost fell over at the sound of the voice. It was the same voice they had heard in the Garden, but this time it ricocheted like thunder across a canyon.

The earth convulsed. Abraham's hand sprang open. *KLAaaangh!* The knife rang out as it fell on the rock.

"Do not touch the lad. Don't lay a hand on him!" the voice called out. "Now I *know* that you believe and trust me."

Abraham fumbled at the knots to release his son.

Suddenly there was a noise in the bramble bushes right beside Derek. A ram was grazing. Deeper and deeper it pressed into the bush, seeking tender morsels. A branch snapped. His horns were caught. Immediately, the mountaintop was engulfed by sounds of bleating and thrashing as the ram writhed free itself. It twisted, trying to butt Derek with his head, but his horns were caught.

"Move!" Yaldar commanded quietly, pointing to his right. "We can't let them see us here."

Yaldar's command distracted Derek just long enough for the ram to score one powerful kick with his hind leg, sending Derek careening down the hillside, writhing and grasping at his already wounded leg.

At least I'm out of sight, he thought as he limped to join Phoebe and Yaldar behind a rock outcropping.

Abraham was still shaking. He just wanted to embrace his son, but that had to wait. "Elohim provided!" Abraham shouted, pressing his fists at the sky. "He has given me back my son."

Father and son looked at each other for a brief moment, then rushed to take hold of the ram before it could get away. They dragged it, protesting and kicking, to the altar where they tied it with the same ropes that had so recently bound Isaac.

Abraham stared at the ram through his tears. This time he raised his knife without hesitation. The blade flashed bright red in the sunlight as it sliced the throat of the sacrifice.

Together father and son embraced and kissed each other's cheeks as they watched lifeblood flow out of the ram over the rock and onto the ground. Abraham struck his flint, just as he had rehearsed. A spark lit the kindling, which in turn ignited the wood on the altar, creating the blaze that consumed the sacrifice. Isaac's life has been spared.

Derek and Phoebe could hear the old man repeat to his son, "The promise is true."

Yaldar, Phoebe, and Derek stood speechless as they watched Abraham and Isaac walk slowly down the mountain together.

"Derek," Yaldar said. "There will be a few strands of the rope that will work for us. Get a couple of them and meet us at the entrance to the cave."

Derek approached the embers, searching for anything not burned to a crisp. He scanned the scene for some red remnant. On the ground were two strands of the rope, now red with the blood of the sacrifice. He trembled a bit as he picked them up.

Entering the cave, he handed the strands to Phoebe, who was standing with Yaldar. They all watched the fibers entwine themselves with Phoebe's wristband.

"Before they entered the cave, Yaldar turned to Derek and Phoebe and said, "We are standing at one of the holiest places on earth. Many people believe that the Anointed One, the Messiah, will come to this place at the end of days. When we began today, this was just another mountain. From this time forward, it is a central part of the history of the world."

10

THE MASTERPIECE

Workshop

Inside the cave, Yaldar tapped his staff to the ground. The red dot revealed the portal, which began to grow and open.

As soon as Phoebe saw Sophia waiting for them on the other side, she stepped through. Derek and Yaldar followed.

"That was intense," Phoebe said. She grabbed Sophia and hugged her. "He was going to kill his own son."

"I know," Sophia said somberly.

"Why would God possibly ask him to do that?"

"Yeah," Derek chimed in, "why?"

"Do you remember the picture about this from Istanbul? In the Church?"

"Sure," Derek said. "It was the father sacrificing his son, and the ram was in the background. We were there. So God did provide."

"And?" the weaver pressed.

"But not until Abraham was just about to kill Isaac," Derek answered.

"So here is a question for you: What did Abraham believe?" Sophia challenged.

"He believed that God could do the impossible," Derek said. "And I guess he believed that God would raise Isaac from the dead somehow, right? Because otherwise the first promises would never be true, and God can't lie. Also, Isaac had to believe, didn't he?"

Sophia smiled gently and motioned toward her worktable. On it was the faded weaving of Mount Moriah.

"It's all so faded and colorless," Phoebe lamented.

"Let me see your wrist," Sophia said. When Phoebe extended her arm, the thread gently released into the open hands of the weaver, who held it close.

Phoebe furrowed her brow and pursed her lips. "There is no place in this picture for the thread!" she complained. " The panel depicts the scene with Isaac on the altar. He did not die. There is no red. Don't tell me we went through all of that, and you don't need the thread. That's not right. What I see is Isaac on the rock and Abraham standing over him with his knife in the air. The angel is in the background. And the knife is falling out of Abraham's wide-open hand. The ram is caught in those bushes, but there is no blood."

"Did you see the blood when you were there?" Sophia asked.

"Yeah, lots of it. Everywhere. But not until the ram was killed," Derek answered.

"And what was the ram?"

"A sacrifice. He took Isaac's place on the altar," Derek replied.

"The story is about the blood, even though you can't see it from the front of the Tapestry," Sophia explained. She turned the panel over and fed the thread into the reverse. Then she showed the front. All of the colors were brilliantly restored. The sky was blue. The foliage was green. The angel was white, and the thorn bushes were dusty green. Abraham's beard was white, and their faces were just as the kids remembered. There was blood. The thread was very clear in the reverse.

"I get it," Derek said. "The power is felt even when it is not seen."

Sophia smiled approvingly. Later she offered her guests some tea with bread, cheese, and hummus. "Now you must go to the richest country in the world," she said to the kids.

"America?" Derek asked.

Sophia and Yaldar laughed.

THE TEN PLAGUES

1 WATERS TURNED TO BLOOD
2 FROGS
3 INSECTS
4 WILD ANIMALS
5 DISEASE & PESTILENCE
6 BOILS
7 HAIL
8 LOCUSTS
9 DARKNESS
10 DEATH OF THE FIRSTBORN MALE

III

CONFRONTATION

c. 1500 BC

"Welcome," Yaldar proclaimed as he spread his arms and led Derek and Phoebe through the portal.

Phoebe's eyes widened as she looked at her brother. He was dressed in white linen woven from Egyptian flax. He wore a gold collar around his neck. On his head was a woven blue headband with an amber stone in the center. His white kilt was short like most of the men, and his short white vest, with its red and blue border, revealed his bare chest.

"Derek, is that really you?" Phoebe asked in disbelief.

She, too, felt the dramatic change in her clothing. Her linen dress was white and sheath-like. It went nearly to her ankles and was suspended on her shoulders by two wide straps. She also had a wide, gold collar. Her hair was long and black and squared off midway down her back, and her forehead was framed with bangs. It was all held in place by a white headband with a red jewel in its center.

"Wow, Phoebes," Derek said. "You really look beautiful. I don't know what kind of party this is, but I'm glad we made it. Even our sandals are styling."

"This is ritzy and we are dressed for success. We fit right in. Even you, Yaldar. How do you do it?"she asked. "You don't change, but you look absolutely regal here."

"We have just traveled back in time over three thousand years," Yaldar explained. "The sculptures and art on the walls depict Pharaoh Ramses as a god and celebrate his victories. Don't you love cave travel?"

A servant girl passed by with a plate of figs. "Thanks," Derek said, reaching for a handful.

Phoebe flashed a look just like their mom's. He took one fig and smiled. The girl bowed her head to demonstrate her low station, but her eyes sparkled when they met Derek's.

"Really, this feels like we are at a resort and we are getting ready for a huge party," Derek observed.

"Not so much," replied Phoebe. "Look at their faces. There is not one smile among them. It's more like the last party on the *Titanic*," she whispered.

"This is quite the palace. I get all the sandy desert in Egypt, but where did all that water out there come from?" Derek asked.

"That's the Nile River," Yaldar replied. "It is the longest river in the world. We are standing in the palace of the ruler Pharaoh Ramses. All of Egypt worships him as a god. And, yes, it's ritzy. By now Egypt has been the richest country in the world for over 1500 years."

"I thought Egypt was a poor country," Phoebe said.

"It will be," Yaldar replied. "Right now, the Nile has the power to feed the world as they know it, from Spain to Arabia and everywhere in between."

"Things are about to change," Yaldar said, turning his head to look down the river. The crowd went silent when a pair of triangular white sails were spotted zigzagging up the river.

Everyone stood in silence when the small feluccas approached the dock. Eyes were glued on the two old men who got out of the wooden boat first. Tension hung in the air. The Egyptian upper class shuffled nervously.

Moses.

He wore a threadbare black robe and sandals that were barely more than scraps of leather.

"With him is his brother, Aaron, and the elders of the Hebrew tribes," Yaldar explained, "In the eyes of Pharaoh, Moses has single-handedly destroyed their economy and ruined the life of the rich here. Amazingly, he is very well respected by the servants and common people."

A young member of Pharaoh's guard confronted Derek. "We are still in charge here. There is nothing left for him but to go back to the desert. Pharaoh will be rid of him soon enough."

"The contrast is amazing. It's a showdown," Phoebe whispered. "The wealthy Egyptians are all afraid. Even then, shouldn't Moses dress up for an audience with the king?"

"The desert has not been kind to Moses during his exile," Yaldar answered.

Guess not, thought Phoebe. *Moses looks completely unequal to his task.* "How many years ago was Moses banished into the desert?" she asked.

"Forty. Everybody here knows the story. As a baby, Moses was rescued from the Nile and raised like the Prince of Egypt. He could have been second to the Pharaoh himself. Then there was a day when Moses lost it. He killed an Egyptian for abusing a Hebrew slave. He didn't think anybody saw him, but the word got out. Moses fled to the desert to save his life. He should probably be dead by now. After all, he's about eighty years old."

"He's ba-ack," Derek quipped.

"Were Moses and Pharaoh friends then?" asked Phoebe.

"We don't know, but they are mortal enemies now. That's for sure," replied Yaldar.

"What do you mean, *mortal*? Nobody has died."

"Stick around," Yaldar said, his eyes rolling.

Tall pillars rose beside Pharaoh's throne, which was covered in gold and jewels. Pharaoh's feet were always above the heads of the people. At Pharaoh's right was a similar but smaller throne for the crown prince. The guests all had to look up as they watched their ruler make his grand entrance.

Ten brass trumpets on either side of the stage announced the arrival of Pharaoh. He was arrayed in garments of white silk embroidered with golden images of the gods. He wore heavy golden necklaces and bracelets. On his head was a golden headdress bearing the scarab and the cobra, the symbols of Upper and Lower Egypt. His golden staff was capped with the golden image of a cobra with ruby red eyes. Even his sandals flashed with gold.

"Hail to Pharaoh, ruler of all Egypt," the people proclaimed. Pharaoh was followed closely by his young son, the crown prince. They strode into the grand hall, receiving the prescribed adoration from the people. Pharaoh sat down first, then his son. There was no seating for the bystanders. From his golden throne, he glared disgustedly at the old man and the chiefs of the slave families.

The hall became deathly silent.

Moses, Aaron, and the elders of Israel took their time walking across the great stone court and up to the base of Pharaoh's exalted throne where their eyes were directly at the level of Ramses feet.

They did not bow.

"He has been here nine times," Yaldar whispered. "So far nine plagues have ruined Egypt as they know it. The Nile was turned to blood. It killed all of the fish. Animals and crops have been destroyed. Hailstones, boils . . . pretty much anything that can go wrong."

Moses stood silent while Aaron's voice boomed through the great hall. "The God of the Hebrews says: 'Let my people go!' "

"If you do not let the people go, every firstborn male in Egypt, whether human or animal, will die at midnight tonight," Aaron proclaimed.

Moses fixed his gaze on Pharaoh's son. Derek shuddered as he contemplated the meaning of the moment.

"We will take all of our cattle and possessions with us," Aaron continued. "Tomorrow we will go worship the Lord."

"Whoa. You can cut the air with a knife," Derek gasped.

The crowd around Derek and Phoebe was frozen with fear. "Firstborn male?" Derek and Phoebe heard the bystanders say.

"Midnight." The word rippled through the crowd.

"What can we do?" Phoebe asked. "They can't escape, can they?"

Moses' determined gaze saddened as he looked back at Pharaoh's son.

* * *

The gathering watched Moses, Aaron, and the elders walk out of the palace, board the felucca, and set sail down the Nile.

"This way," Yaldar said, leading Derek and Phoebe into the dark recesses of the palace.

"Wait a minute," Derek protested. "We did not get a thread. We can't leave yet."

"We are not finished," Yaldar replied, tapping his staff three times rapidly on the marble floor. The red dot appeared and the portal almost instantly expanded to its full size. "We are not going far in time or distance, but you need a change of clothes," Yaldar explained. "You are not upper-class Egyptians anymore."

12

PASSOVER

c. 1500 BC

The portal disappeared as quickly as it had come. "Hot," Phoebe said, feeling the sizzling sand through the soles of her thin sandals.

"Slaves don't get nice shoes," Yaldar replied.

"How do you say, 'designer gunny sack?' " Phoebe quipped. "It's itchy."

"With a little brown headscarf, you are good to go," chuckled Yaldar, producing a square of cloth. "Welcome to Goshen, the Hebrew slave region of Egypt."

Derek wore a plain wool kilt with a rope belt and no shirt. He also wore thin sandals and a headscarf.

While Derek and Phoebe walked down a sandy street, a woman came rushing out of her house. "What are you doing in the street?" she cried. "You are not safe here. Come with me. My name is Tabitha," she said. She scurried her two small children, along with Derek and Phoebe, into her tiny dwelling.

Their eyes dashed nervously as they entered her mud-brick dwelling. "Almost like an adobe house in New Mexico," Phoebe whispered.

"Did you feel that?" Derek asked. "The wind and the animals are restless. What's going on?"

"I feel it too," Phoebe whispered.

Yaldar was nowhere to be found.

"Why were you in the streets?" a woman called out as she ran toward Derek and Phoebe. "Moses has sent word. There is another plague coming. This time God will strike dead the firstborn males, whether they are human or animals. Before, we Hebrews were protected from the plagues. This time is different. Our firstborn males could die, too, if we don't do what Moses says. Tonight we will kill a lamb and roast it."

We must eat it all. "We have enough for our neighbor, Amnon, but he has refused to come. He thinks Moses is on some kind of power trip. This is my husband, Hesed," Tabitha continued. It wasn't an introduction, just information. "Help him. He will show you what to do," she said to Derek.

"You can help me," she said, tugging Phoebe's sleeve. "Cut up these vegetables. Then we will dice bitter herbs, horseradish, and grind up a hummus mixture." She took a lump of dough and led Phoebe out to the men.

Beside the firepit was a brick dome about waist high. "We do not have time for our bread to rise," she said. "Flatten this lump with your hands and place it on sidewall of the oven, like this," she said. It will bake quickly." Then we will peel it off with this." She held up a flat wooden spatula.

Kinda like a pizza oven, Phoebe thought.

Behind the house a lamb was tied to a stake near their fire pit. "Grab his hind legs," Hesed ordered as he simultaneously took hold of the head and released the rope. Derek held each leg tightly and tried to prevent the sacrifice from kicking. Hesed and Derek lifted the animal up onto a good-sized rock. Derek felt the warm flesh of the unsuspecting lamb.

From a distance, Phoebe watched Hesed draw his knife. He examined the blade to be sure that it was sharp and then, with a single, quick stroke, sliced the neck.

Blood spurted everywhere. Derek's hands felt life oozing from its body until it was completely still.

"Lift him up! By the legs," Hesed snapped. "Don't you know how to bleed out an animal?" He grabbed the animal's hind legs and tied them off, high enough to drain out all of the blood. He glared at Derek, but there was no time for reprimanding.

"Fill that bowl," Hesed called to Phoebe, who could not believe what she was about to do, but she dutifully bent down to collect the blood flowing from the lamb.

With his knife Hesed dressed the hanging animal.

"Kinda like we saw in Eden, isn't it?" Derek whispered to Phoebe.

"When I was your age, I had butchered hundreds of animals. Haven't you ever seen a lamb killed?"

"Once," Derek replied.

"Who are these kids?" Hesed mumbled under his breath.

Artfully, he pierced the lifeless body with a sharp stick and hung it over the fire. Then he pointed to the bowl with the blood of the lamb. "Bring it," he directed. Derek picked it up and, with his sister, carefully followed him to the front door of the house.

Three large stalks of hyssop were blooming nearby. "This is what Moses told us to use for a paintbrush." Hesed dipped the small white flowers into the bowl. They turned bright red, soaking up the still-warm blood. "It works," he said.

Then he handed one stalk to Phoebe, one to Derek, and kept one for himself. "Like this," he said, brushing the stalk against the doorframe. "The message from Moses was to put the blood of the lamb on the doorposts and the lintle of the house."

He pointed to one doorpost for Phoebe and took the other himself. "Since you are the tallest," he said to Derek, "you get the top." There was no way Derek could prevent blood from sprinkling onto his headscarf and his tunic as he painted the beam above the doorway.

"What about him?" Derek asked, pointing to a neighbor standing smugly with his son, outside his house.

"Ask him," replied Hesed.

"Aren't you sacrificing?" Derek called out.

"Naw. It's all a trick to get everyone to commit to Moses. I'm not doing it," he said as he shook his head. "Not gonna happen."

Derek and Phoebe froze when they heard his answer.

Hesed nervously scanned the rest of the neighbors. "Get inside," he ordered as he checked their work and secured the door.

"All is ready," announced Tabitha.

Hesed sat on a small cushion while Derek sat on the ground beside him. Phoebe helped Tabitha carry the large brass tray. The whole lamb—head, eyes, and all—was surrounded by vegetables and bitter herbs. The flatbread was thin as a cracker and lacked aroma and flavor. Tabitha sat opposite Hesed, with Derek and Phoebe between them on one side and the children on the other.

"Blessed be the Lord, King of the universe," Hesed prayed. The sun dipped below the horizon. The skies became turbulent. "Eat quickly," he insisted. "We must eat the whole lamb tonight and move out in the morning."

Derek winced when he looked at the eyeball. He had heard
that in some cultures it was a delicacy given to a guest. *Please, no,*
he thought.

At midnight, wind from the desert began to howl. The
windows and doors shook. It started low but soon grew loud.

Then came the screams. "EYIeeeeee! EYIeeeeee!"

Voices pierced the night. Screams of disbelief turned to fear
and despair.

"We have to help them!" Derek shouted. He jumped up and
darted for the doorway.

"No!" cried Hesed, tackling him like an NFL linebacker.

"You cannot go out there," Tabitha's voice penetrated the
darkness.

"Why not?" Derek replied. "Somebody ought to help. And
I really—"

"No!" Tabitha protested, standing between Derek and the
door. She got right in his face.

"This is your sister? Yes?" Tabitha pointed to Phoebe.

"Yes," answered Derek sheepishly.

"And you are the firstborn male of your family?"

"Yes," he responded with growing trepidation.

"Then do you want to die tonight? That's what your curiosity
will get you. If you go outside this door, you will die!"

Derek sat down and did not say another word.

"This night is different from all the others," she said. "You
must always remember."

"Tomorrow, we will begin a new life. We will go with Moses
to the land promised to our ancestors, Abraham, Isaac and Jacob."

When the morning sun struck the adobe hut, Hesed cautiously opened the door. The streets were filling with neighbors checking on one another and gathering their belongings to follow Moses.

When Derek and Phoebe finally walked outside, they saw the branches of hyssop lying beside the doorway. Instinctively, Phoebe picked up the branch she had used the night before and turned it thoughtfully in her hands.

In the distance Derek spotted Yaldar's hat above the crowd. They quickly made their way to him.

"Why did you leave us?" Phoebe asked.

"Now it is *your* Passover," he replied.

Phoebe looked down at the hyssop branch in her hand.

"Bring it," said Yaldar. He led them away from the village to a new wall under construction. "Hebrew slaves would normally have been working there, but now there are no Hebrew slaves."

Phoebe took one final look back at the home of Hesed and Tabitha. Next door they saw Amnon on his knees, cradling his son's lifeless body.

"Will he go with Moses?" Derek asked.

"Hard to say. Right now he is very angry with Moses."

Yaldar led Phoebe and Derek to a remote spot and tapped the ground. The red dot appeared on the wall. The portal grew to its wobbly, oval form. Sophia was waiting for them.

13

HYSSOP

~~~

Workshop

"*Ah*, my darlings. What have you brought this time?" Sophia asked.

Phoebe presented the stalk with its blood-stained flowers.

"Hyssop!" Sophia exclaimed. "Of course. Let's go to the table."

"It's from the Passover. We painted the doorposts with it," Phoebe said.

"Yes, dear," Sophia replied, turning the hyssop stalk and cherishing the once-white flowers. "This is the blood of your Passover Lamb. Well done."

"I never saw anything die before," Derek said, "I felt it die in my own hands. The lifeblood drained out on the ground. It was warm and still. Then we roasted it and ate it all."

On Sophia's table was a long, shallow bowl with water and a single white thread lying on the bottom. Sophia drew the thread out and handed it to Derek.

"This strand is linen," she explained. "It is made from the flax plants grown in fields along the Nile. In this bowl we will transfer blood of the lamb."

With that she took the stalk from Phoebe and dipped the blood-drenched hyssop flowers into the water.

Immediately the bright red color was drawn from the flowers into the water until the flowers were completely white again. Carefully, she dipped the flax thread into the water. They watched in amazement as the color migrated into the strand. When Sophia lifted one end high in the air, she handed it back to Derek. Then she ran her hand along the thread, squeezing out any excess water.

"The water is clear. There is nothing on Sophia's hands. All of the color transferred to the thread," Phoebe whispered.

Sophia reached across her table and found the panel she wanted. "This is Passover," she said. She threaded a large wooden needle and picked up her weaver's comb. Gently, she guided the thread into the tapestry. Back and forth, Sophia worked the needle as the kids watched the red thread reveal the doorposts of Hesed and Tabitha's house. As they had seen before, blue, green, and gold colors began to reveal themselves. Then she handed the kids the finished panel.

"Tea?" Sophia offered.

14

THE HOLY ARK

One Year after Egypt
(c. 1499 BC)

"**B**ats!" Yaldar shouted as the portal closed behind them. "Duck!" He pushed Derek and Phoebe out of the flight path of hundreds of noisy creatures flapping their wings and flying erratically.

"Are they bats or ducks?" Derek teased.

"Okay, you got me," Yaldar replied. "They're bats. Just don't go any deeper into the cave."

"Why not?" Derek probed.

"There's guano in there. Bat poop. It has been accumulating in these caves for centuries, and you don't want to step in it."

"Get us out of here, Yaldar!" Phoebe reacted. "This is disgusting . . . and smelly too. Are you sure this is the right way?" When she spotted a flickering yellow light at the mouth of the cave, she rushed toward it.

Derek decided not to touch the cave wall. "Volcanic, I think." Then he said, "Something's burning out there. It looks like a whirling tower of fire."

"Right you are," Yaldar replied. "It is the Pillar of Fire, and it has led the Hebrew people from Egypt to this place. Whenever the pillar moves, the people follow. All night it stands guard as a fire. Now watch: as the sun rises it will change."

After a few minutes Phoebe's jaw dropped. "Sure enough!" she exclaimed. "The fire has gone out. It's still a pillar, but now it's a pillar of cloud. The only cloud in the sky. Amazing!"

"It will be a cloud until nightfall, then it will become a fire again," said Yaldar. "It will happen every day until they get to the promised land."

Just beyond the pillar, a black mountain loomed over the sprawling Hebrew encampment. "That is Mount Sinai," Yaldar informed his travelers, "where Moses has been meeting with Yahweh. He was called and commissioned up there. The Ten Commandments were delivered up there. The Law was given there, and so much more."

As the sun rose, its rays reflected off two metallic objects in the center of the camp. "That is what we have come here to see," Yaldar said. "They call it the Tabernacle. It is their moveable temple, and today is the day for its dedication."

The Tabernacle was bordered by a giant rectangular courtyard consisting of white woven curtains about ten feet tall. The curtains took on the golden glow of the morning. The sun reflected off the large bronze object and then behind it a sat smaller one. Near the opposite end of the courtyard was a large rectangular tent.

"Let's go see it," Phoebe suggested.

When they neared the encampment, the travelers were confronted by a soldier who stood motionless, but the threat of the spear in his hands made them stop. The man was tall and broad-shouldered, with a dense black beard. His dark eyes seemed to penetrate Derek and Phoebe, yet there was a genuine kindness in his voice. Even Phoebe let down her guard just a bit.

"Who are you?" the guard inquired.

"I am Yaldar, and these are my fellow travelers, Derek and Phoebe. We are here on a quest."

The guard studied Yaldar carefully. "I recognize you. Last year I saw you in the Palace of Pharaoh, right?" he asked.

"Yes," Yaldar agreed.

"I am Joshua, a commander of the guard of Israel. What is your quest?"

"We must restore a Tapestry," Derek said.

Phoebe did not respond. She had noticed something white covering the ground. "Did it snow here last night?" she asked. "Is that even possible in the desert? Just look, everywhere people are gathering up that white stuff, and they are taking it back to their tents."

She picked up some of the substance and sniffed it. "Feels kinda crunchy."

"Taste it," Joshua urged.

"Ew," she said, holding it away and shaking her head. "It smells a little funny."

"Go on, taste it," Joshua encouraged. He picked up a piece and popped it into his mouth.

Tentatively, Phoebe bit into it and then wrinkled up her face. "What is it?"

"Ha," Yaldar said, laughing. "You are correct . . . in a way. It's called manna, and in the language of the Hebrews, manna means 'what is it?' So your question is your answer." Yaldar chuckled. "Nobody knows what it is, but what we know is that this manna will feed our people as long as we are here in this desert land."

"Can't say it's tasty, but I feel a little fuller," Phoebe replied.

"We boil it, we bake it, and we get tired of it," Joshua agreed. "But you're right. It fills us up."

Just then another man came striding up to the group. He was rather mysterious in his ways and seemed almost to float above the ground as he walked.

"Yaldar!" the man called out, spreading his arms wide.

"Bez," Yaldar responded, immediately, while bracing himself for a giant bear hug.

"I am so glad you are here, my friend, and today of all days. Your timing is perfect," the man declared.

"Excellent!" Yaldar replied. "Just as I planned, and I have brought important guests with me. Allow me to introduce Derek and his sister Phoebe. They are on a quest to restore a Tapestry, and your tabernacle is a part of it."

The encounter surprised Joshua. He turned to Bezalel and spoke very gruffly. "What are you doing out here? They say that you are not finished yet."

"Soon," Bezalel replied.

Joshua flashed Bezalel an unconvinced look. "There are only about five hours before the ceremony. Everything is ready except you. You should have been finished days ago. The ceremonies will begin at exactly noon today. The music, food, and sacrifices are prepared. What are you doing way out here? This is for Passover! The appointed day. We have no margin for error!"

"I just had to get away and think. It won't take long to finish," reassured Bezalel.

"Well, Yahweh can't wait," Joshua replied with a stern gaze. "I have things to do . . . and so do you." He pivoted and headed back into the encampment.

"Just be —" Bez started to say *patient*, but instead he just stood silently watching Joshua disappear among the array of tents.

"Call me Bez. I needed a little time. I can't rush the ark," he tried to explain. "After all, it's the most important thing in the whole tabernacle."

"The ark? As in Raiders?" Derek said excitedly.

"What is raiders?" Bezalel looked puzzled.

Derek winced.

"Just a story," Yaldar interjected, flashing a stern look at Derek.

Derek decided to start over. "What is the ark?"

"It is the place where Yahweh will meet with His people." Bezalel replied. "I am in charge of the entire tabernacle project, and the ark is the focal point of everything here." Bez was wiry and animated to say the least. His bright eyes flashed intensely. His hands were huge and strong, with very muscular forearms. His hair was wild, yet there was something very soft and sensitive about him.

Has anybody ever seen the ark?" Phoebe asked.

"Yes, I have seen it," Bezalel replied. "I first saw it in my mind when Moses told me Yahweh's instructions. Then I really saw it when it took form in my own hands. You see, I made it . . . almost."

"Almost?" Phoebe furrowed her brow.

"I'm not quite finished," Bez replied. "I just had to get away to get one last burst of inspiration. When I approach the ark, I feel its power, and it scares me even now. You see, it is the place where Yahweh's presence will dwell with our people. After I am finished, anybody who touches it will die. I am almost afraid to finish it."

Phoebe became exasperated. "Do you really think Yahweh would give you enough talent to get this far, and not enough to finish?" she protested. She put her hands on her hips and gave him her best "snap out of it" stare.

Bezalel was stunned. "You're right," he replied. A change came over his face. "Whenever we worked on it, we felt Yahweh's pleasure. We all felt His Spirit guiding us as we fashioned it. It is the finest sculpture I have ever made. I had never seen angel's wings until I saw them being formed in my own hands. Of course, it will be His pleasure for me to finish it. Let's go. I'm ready now."

"So, a tapestry has brought you here," he said as they walked. "Just wait until you see our great curtains. We call them veils. They are awesome tapestries, decorated with cherub-angels and pomegranates of red, blue, and purple. Our best weavers have fashioned them, and they are masterpieces."

Bez studied his visitors as a sculptor might look at a model, taking note of Phoebe's dark hair, bright eyes, and broad smile and Derek's warrior-like physique. Then he grinned and pointed the way into the camp, walking at a pace that forced Derek and Phoebe to hustle. Somehow Yaldar easily matched him stride for stride. When they reached the tabernacle, Bez pulled back the curtain so that they could see into the courtyard.

"There are two veils in the tabernacle, and they are elegant tapestries. The one you see can covers the entrance to the Holy Place. The one you don't see is inside and separates the ark from everything else. It is the most wondrous veil our weavers have ever made."

"I want to see it," Derek said.

"Off limits!" Bez insisted. "Except for our artisans. In fact, this is the last day anyone other than a priest can look inside our new tabernacle . . . and live. Look at the first veil. Even from here you can see the intricacies of cherub-angels, pomegranates, and bells."

"Isn't that a little much for a tent here in this desert?" Derek asked.

"Everything here is the design of Yahweh. It is supposed to be over the top—the very best!"

"All this for a God who tells you not to make any statue, even to Him?" Derek asked.

"Not a statue, of or to Him, but a place *for* Him. We know about images. In Egypt we were forced to make statues and idols for the Pharaohs," Bez explained. "We made images of jackals and bugs and birds of all kinds. Some had human bodies with heads of animals. But they have no powers. I made them. I know. Then some of our artisans made a golden calf right here in the desert. We know better. Why would anyone want to bow down to an image if they made it themselves? Makes no sense. Yahweh is beyond what I can imagine or think."

"So, what is in the ark?" Derek asked.

"Miracles, you could say. We put three things inside the box before we put the cover on it. First is the Ten Commandments engraved by the finger of Yahweh on stone tablets. Then there is a pot of manna that provides for the people. You tasted it this morning." Bez looked at Phoebe questioningly and she nodded. "It feeds us every day. Nobody gets sick. Nobody gets hungry, and nobody knows what it is. And also there is the staff of Aaron, the High Priest."

"The golden cover is what I have to finish. It is solid gold, and it is where the High Priest will sprinkle the blood of the sacrificed animal. I am sculpting two solid gold cherub angels that sit on top like witnesses to the sacrifice and forgiveness of the sins of the people." Bez paused reflectively, then continued, "We will do it every year because . . . well, you understand. It is only for past sins."

Bez was always checking out the workmanship and looking for anything that might not be perfect. When he saw a single loose red thread on the curtain of the entrance, he carefully removed it.

"Here," he said, handing it to Phoebe. "A souvenir. Maybe for your Tapestry?" Not to her surprise, the thread gently wound itself around her wrist.

Well, then, I must finish now," Bezalel said, giving a bear hug to each of his guests and wishing them shalom before disappearing into the gathering throng.

Phoebe and Derek stood and watched the desert "bloom" as the people began to show up dressed in their best desert attire. Everybody had prepared.

Suddenly, from the center of the camp a loud sound blasted.

"What's that?" Phoebe asked. "It sounds like a trumpet."

"That is the shofar, the ram's horn that calls the people together," Yaldar said. "Moses and Aaron will be arriving soon. The one with the jeweled breastplate is Aaron, the High Priest. Today is Passover. This ceremony will go for days. There will be sacrifices, prayers, and feasting. We will only watch for a short while."

Derek and Phoebe stood motionless beside Yaldar while a bull was brought in before Moses, Aaron, and many priests, all of whom laid their hands on it. Moses' prayer was very long. Derek fidgeted until, with a single stroke, a priest sliced the neck of the bull. It collapsed and its blood flowed. Some poured onto the ground, and some was captured in bowls and splashed by the priests onto the sides of the brass altar.

I can't get close enough to get blood from the sacrifice," Derek complained. "What are we going to do?"

We have what we need," Yaldar answered. He looked at Bez's gift wrapped around Phoebe's wrist. "It's enough."

At the cave entrance, Yaldar looked back on the encampment. In the distance were the sounds of trumpets and tambourines. The smoky fires of the burnt offerings were ascending into the sky, and Mount Sinai stood nobly in the background.

Slowly the pillar of cloud positioned itself above the tabernacle, right over Holy of Holies and the Ark of the Covenant.

"Yahweh is going to dwell with His people," said Yaldar.

15

ROPE AND BELLS

Workshop

With the tap of Yaldar's staff, the portal fully opened. Phoebe and Derek peered through to the other side but didn't see anyone.

"Where is Sophia?" Phoebe asked. "She is always here. What's happened? Are you sure we are in the right place? Yaldar, are we even in the right time?"

A cold flash went through her. *What if we can't get back to our dad after all?*

Just then Sophia came into view and extended her arms to the kids. Derek and Phoebe quickly stepped through the portal and hugged her. Yaldar followed quietly.

"What do you have for me this time, my darlings?" she asked.

Phoebe pulled the thread from around her wrist and handed it to Sophia.

"Bez gave this to us. Also, we saw the first sacrifice for the Tabernacle," Derek exclaimed. "Moses and Aaron were standing right there. We looked right in the eye of the bull just as they cut his throat. Blood shot everywhere. They threw its blood on the altar, then they cut it up and placed the parts on the altar too."

"Are you starting to see a pattern here?" Sophia asked.

"Yeah," Phoebe responded. "Everywhere we go something dies."

"Yes," Sophia said, smiling. "And now we can restore this panel." Then she located the weaving with the ark and positioned it on her table.

Derek was surprised when Sophia handed the thread to him. The texture was softer than he had imagined, and very fine. He turned it between his thumb and forefinger. When he touched it to the panel, it began moving smoothly through his fingers and into the fabric. "It's like the thread is alive."

"Look how the color comes back," Phoebe gushed. "There is the blood on the brass altar in the courtyard. I see the High Priest standing at the veil with the ark in front of him."

"We didn't see the ark," said Derek. "I really wanted to see it."

"Me too," echoed Phoebe.

The brilliant colors of the tabernacle filled in first. Finally, the ark shimmered bright gold as if it emitted its own light.

Derek turned to Yaldar, who was standing quietly in the background. "I have a question for you. When I was waiting for them to kill the bull, I saw some other priests tie a rope around the ankle of Aaron. Why did they do that?"

"Good observation. Did you happen to hear anything when Aaron was walking?"

"I heard little bells ringing," Derek offered.

"Did you notice the hem of Aaron's robe, by any chance?"

"Yeah, I saw the gold bells and little red pomegranates. What are they for?"

"The bells announce the High Priest before he walks to the Holy of Holies. Of course, nobody really sneaks up on God, but it is appropriate to be announced. And the rope? From the beginning, there was a concern that the High Priest might not be worthy enough to represent the people and would be struck dead in the presence of the Almighty. As a precaution, they tied that rope around his ankle so they could drag him out if he died. If the bells went silent for too long, they would know," Yaldar explained.

"Did it ever get used?"

"Nobody knows. Maybe," Yaldar replied.

"I have a surprise for you," Sophia said the following morning. "A caravan arrived, and I bought some eggs, tomatoes, and yogurt. Also, the peaches arrived from Avanos. They are in season now, and so delicious. And I have baked our special cave flatbread for you."

"This is great, Sophia," Derek declared. "I think I could eat a horse." She flashed a confused look at him. "Not a real horse!" Derek said. "I just mean a lot of food. It's an expression."

Sophia shrugged, then asked, "Do you ever make predictions?"

"Once I predicted I would get straight As," Derek replied.

"And?"

"Didn't work out so well."

"You can control the input but not the outcome, right?" she asked. "So the outcome would have to be the same, or it wouldn't be a real prediction?"

"Guess so," Derek responded. "So what?"

"Next, Yaldar will take you to a place where predictions are stored. What you must find out is if the predictions were made *before* the event."

"If the predictions aren't made before the event, they aren't predictions, are they?" Phoebe winked.

"Off with you now. I will get other panels ready for you while you are gone."

Yaldar's staff hit the floor, and the kids immediately pivoted and located the red dot on the cave wall. It felt like they had the rhythm now. As soon as the full height was reached, Derek stepped through, followed by Phoebe and Yaldar.

16

QUMRAN

~~~

AD 1946

*I*n the darkness Derek scraped his ankle against a rock "Ow!
This tunnel is so narrow," Derek said.

Yaldar bent down to maneuver through the tight cave tunnel
but did not comment.

"What did Sophia mean by storing up predictions? How is
that possible?" Phoebe asked.

"Follow me and you will see," Yaldar replied.

We can't see anything," Phoebe complained, reaching out
her hands to feel the side walls. "You're blocking what little light
your staff puts out."

"The way might be dark, but I am still leading you, and you
can still follow me, right?"

"Yeah, and I *still* don't like it," she complained.

"Have you ever made a time capsule? Yaldar asked.

"Yes," Phoebe replied. "When they built our new school, we
buried a time capsule inside the cornerstone of the building."

"So what did you put in it?" Yaldar asked.

"A couple of our favorite movies on DVD, a CD by Taylor
Swift, and one of our school yearbooks," recalled Phoebe. "Our

teacher contributed an old iPhone. We put in a Snickers bar, a bag of Doritos, and, oh yeah, a copy of our newspaper, the *Arizona Republic* from that day. I remember the lead story; it was about two kids who were lost in the Superstition Mountains. That sounds ironic right now."

"And I gave you a tennis ball and a golf ball," Derek reminded her.

"What was the time capsule for?" Yaldar questioned.

"So people who came after us could see what our life was like at Caliente Middle School," Phoebe responded. "Nobody can open it for at least thirty years. At the right time they will open it and see what we did and what we were interested in."

"Did it predict anything?" Yaldar inquired.

"You mean, like when Jimmy Smith told us he would be President of the United States someday? Now that would really be a thing," groaned Phoebe. "But it didn't make the time capsule. I guess nobody believed that could happen."

"OK, you are about to see the mother of all time capsules. It is about to be discovered in this cave here in modern Israel. The year is 1947," Yaldar stated.

"That's the same year our grandma came to America," Phoebe exclaimed. "That isn't very long ago compared to where we have been."

"Right," Yaldar answered, straightening up as the tunnel opened into a large cave.

Derek stretched and studied the white walls. The predawn light began to filter through the entrance. "Limestone," he mumbled, "is formed by dead crustaceans and other sea life that has been compressed on a sea floor for thousands of years. Smells a little like chalk too."

"You know, the limestone almost seems to intensify the light. It is hotter and drier here than Sophia's workshop," Phoebe observed. "What does this have to do with a time capsule?"

Derek scrambled to see over the piled-up rocks at the cave's mouth. "Nothing but desert down there, and that big lake in the distance. What's it called?" he asked, straining to analyze their surroundings. It sure looks like a good place for a swim. Let's go!" Derek began to clear rocks from the cave's entrance.

"Hold up!" Yaldar cautioned. "First, that water is too salty. All you can really do is float on top. Virtually nothing can live in it. It is saltier than the Great Salt Lake in Utah, and lower than Death Valley. We are at the lowest place on earth, and . . . we are out of time."

A rock whizzed past Derek's head just as Yaldar's staff pulled him out of the line of fire.

Ping. It was an odd sound for a cave. Not the thud you would expect.

"The time capsule has just been located," Yaldar whispered.

"Quite the locator you got there," Derek said, chuckling. He squinted while he scanned the shadows of the cave. "I see a pile of clay jars covered in years of accumulated cave dust, and one of them is cracked open."

"That's it?" Phoebe sounded disappointed." That's the time capsule?"

"Yup," Yaldar nodded.

Voices outside the cave were getting louder.

With his staff and a nod, Yaldar directed Derek and Phoebe back into the recesses of the cave.

They could hear the debris give way under the intruders' feet, creating a small rockslide just outside the cave. Whoever had thrown the rock had heard the jar break. Now they were exploring the cave like pirates looking for buried treasure.

"These are Bedouin teenagers," whispered Yaldar when they entered the cave. "People of the desert. You can tell by their red-and-white head scarves. Their loose white shirts and baggy American Levis tell you that the world is shrinking."

Two boys waited for their eyes to adjust and then went about tracing the trajectory of their rock. From the shadows, Derek and Phoebe could see them trying to locate the source of the ping.

"They must be brothers," Phoebe suggested. "They're built the same and both have the same strong chin and raven black hair. The taller one is probably older."

"Here!" one of the lads said excitedly. "It's some kind of jar, and it's broken open."

The boys took the clay cylinder into the light. It was about three feet tall, a foot in diameter, flat on the bottom, and narrow at the top. The cap was lying on the floor beside it. They dusted off the jar. A beam of sunlight lit the two-thousand-year-old earthen vessel like a spotlight. It was sandy in color. Shadows revealed the horizontal lines left by the potter's hands. As the boys pulled the contents out of the jar, they unfurled a fragmented roll of what appeared to be yellowed paper with writing on it.

"What does it say?" asked the younger.

"How should I know? I can't read," the other replied. "Besides, the writing is not like ours anyway."

Just then the wind started to howl like a banshee.

"Haboob!" the older brother yelled as he looked out of the cave and saw a wall of blowing sand. It was hundreds of feet high and was headed right toward them.

"We have to get home. Now!" he shouted.

And just like that, they wound their headgear to cover their faces and protect their eyes. They took the scroll and left the jar, hastily piling up a few rocks at the entrance to conceal their secret.

"There are lots more jars," Derek heard one of them say. "Maybe there's gold or silver in them. We will return tomorrow."

"Don't say a word. We will take this one to Kando. He knows things."

"These boys have just discovered the Dead Sea Scrolls," Yaldar whispered. "Just like your time capsule, it has been waiting until the right time to be opened. You could say that it has been waiting for your Scientific Age to arrive. We are standing here in modern times: 1947. World War II has just ended. Next year Israel will become a nation for the first time in over two thousand years . . . and the ancient scriptures will be revealed."

"So, what's a haboob?" Derek asked.

"Oh, that's Arabic for big, hairy sandstorm," Yaldar said with a grin.

Derek thought for several moments. "Very interesting, but really, what is the meaning of all of this, Yaldar? There is no story like this in the Bible, is there?"

"You're right. This is not a story *in* the Bible; it is the time capsule *of* the Bible."

"Can you tell how old these are?" Derek asked.

"Around the time of Jesus."

"How can you know that?"

"Carbon dating," Yaldar replied.

"Is there a website for that?" Phoebe quipped, "like carbondating.com? You know, maybe for very old people."

"Ha, good one," Yaldar replied. "Actually, carbon dating is a very scientific radioactive method of dating ancient discoveries. What is important is that most of what is written here is scientifically dated before the birth of Jesus."

❄ ❄ ❄

Suddenly, the dust from the sandstorm filled the cave, obscuring everything.

"Hey Yaldar," Phoebe asked. "Can I tap the staff this time?"

"Sure. If you believe."

"I think so," she replied with self-assurance.

"Okay," Yaldar said, handing her the staff.

She tapped the floor. "I believe," she stated.

This time the dot appeared as a holographic ball suspended in the dust right in front of them. It expanded into an oversized, bright-red oval band. And with a single step, Phoebe, Derek, and Yaldar were through.

It closed and everything was still.

17

THE VOICE

c. AD 30

"Nothing has changed," Derek observed. "We are in exactly the same spot. We didn't go anywhere. This is the same cave. The same jars are over there. But it does *feel* different. Why is that?"

"Time," Yaldar replied as he gently removed the staff from Phoebe's hand. "Time changes everything."

Derek scanned the surroundings again, looking for clues. "Well, the sandstorm *is* over. There are no stones piled up over the entrance. The cave is wide open, and the sun is hotter. There is a village below on the plain. Now there are small farms, crops, and palm trees where we saw a wasteland. The sea looks pretty much the same."

"Yeah, and this cave looks exactly the same?" Phoebe stated.

"Not so fast," Derek replied. "The jars are different. They are shiny. No dust. And half of them are gone."

"Not exactly *gone*," Yaldar said, cocking his head.

"Obviously they are not here," Derek snapped.

"Yet," Yaldar replied. "They are not here *yet*.

"What do you mean by that?"

"Elementary, my dear Derek," Yaldar said with a wink. "Two thousand years, more or less. We are now in the time of Yeshua."

"Who?" Phoebe questioned.

"That is Jesus to you. But here, in this time and in this land, He is known as Yeshua, which in the Hebrew language means *salvation.*

"Okay," Derek said, "but where are the other jars?"

They are still down there, in Qumran, and they need to get moved up here."

Derek and Phoebe took some time to check out their clothing. "Clearly, desert attire has not changed much in two thousand years," quipped Phoebe. "It would be nice if it fit a little better. Anyway, why are we here?"

"You know this cave *is* the time capsule," Yaldar stated. "If it doesn't have all of the right stuff in it, nobody will see the picture. In the village are the other jars that need to be here in this cave. The Torah and the rest of the Old Testament needs to be here. They may need our help. Let's go."

When Derek stepped outside the cave, loose stones gave way and he lost his footing. "Yikes, Yaldar," he called out as he pivoted onto all fours. "I can't stop sliding. The whole hillside is loose."

Yaldar pointed to his left where a path was barely visible. "Over there," he called out. He carefully balanced himself on the narrow path. Phoebe reached out and took his hand to steady herself as they began to walk. Derek continued to scramble and claw his way, sliding across the loose scree of the hillside.

Near the village a few men and boys were standing near a cluster of small mud brick huts.

"Do people really live in these places? They are so tiny," Phoebe marveled.

"Sure do. Whole families in one room. The cooking is all done outside," Yaldar said, pointing to a fire pit and a small dome made of brick. "That's the oven," he said. "Like Egypt."

"Greetings."

Wow! What a voice! Phoebe thought.

Derek, Phoebe, and Yaldar watched the man as he approached from the desert. He was large and very lean. He flashed an extremely broad grin. "I recognize you," he said to Yaldar.

"Shalom and peace," Yaldar said.

Phoebe studied the man closely. He was just *different*. His reddish hair and beard had all of the style of a 1960's hippie. It accentuated every movement of his head. His skin was deeply tanned and weathered by the desert sun and wind.

He ought to wear a headband, at least, Phoebe thought. His tunic was loosely woven from camel hair. His rope belt held the leather pouch around his waist. His well-worn sandals barely protected his feet from the hot desert sands.

Who is that? she thought. *His voice is so deep and resonant. It goes right through you.*

"Yohanan! These are my young friends, Derek and Phoebe. They are on a quest, and I have brought them here to meet you."

"What a pleasure." He grinned and opened his hands widely. "Whatever I can do to help."

"I have never heard a name like Yohanan before," Phoebe whispered to Yaldar. "Are we supposed to recognize him?"

"Yes, but I am not surprised that you do not. His name has not changed but has morphed through time and translation. Listen to the sound. *Yo-ha-nan* sounds a little like *Yo-han* that morphed over time to *Jo-han* and then in English to *John*, as in John . . . the Baptist."

Phoebe turned to Derek and cocked her head as if to say, *Really?*

"Your timing is perfect, my friends," Yohanan continued. "I have been announcing the coming of the Messiah, who will bring peace and judge evil. I warn everyone to clean up their lives before

Messiah arrives. Then I baptize them at the Jordan River, just over there."

"Yohanan," a runner said as he approached. "Romans! There must be over a hundred. We have to hide the scrolls now!"

Faintly in the distance, the sound of horses' hooves and the clatter of chariot wheels on the stone road began an ominous crescendo.

"Quickly," Yohanan directed. "The library."

The inside walls of the huge rectangular hall were lined with large earthen containers, each sealed with a pottery cap.

"The jars are all so very different," Phoebe said when she saw them all lined up against the walls. "That one looks like the one that was broken in the cave. Its base has the same loop handles on the shoulders and the same dark line at the base. Are these the ones that were missing from the cave this morning?"

"Yes," The Voice replied.

Instinctively, Phoebe blurted, "We will help you."

"Which of the jars do we need to take?" Derek asked.

A lad named Natan pointed to a dozen jars that he had marked for the caves.

"Move!" Yohanan called out. "Be sure the lid is secure, then lay it on its side. Use cords to make a sling that will hold the front and back of the jar. We will use poles to sling them on our shoulders. Two of us can carry one jar. Be very careful not to slip on the mountain."

Bending down to prepare a jar, Derek recalled what Yaldar had told them about the predictions.

"Which jar has the Isaiah scroll?" he asked.

Everyone in the room stopped and turned to look.

"It is over there," Yohanan said, pointing to the jar Phoebe had just spotted. "We will get it later."

"Can we take it now?" Phoebe asked.

"Do you know something we don't know, stranger?" Yohanan challenged.

Derek froze. He heard himself say, "There are many mysteries in that scroll. Can we take it now?"

"Sure. You carry it . . . quickly!"

Before they could move, they heard a commotion as the horsemen approached the village. Derek and Phoebe hid and watched as the soldier held his sword to the throat of a villager who promptly surrendered his bunch of bananas. Herod's guards continued, knocking people down, confiscating all kinds of stuff, and threatening the people of the village.

"Romans always terrorize us, just to let off steam. They know we have water, and they take it, even from our sacred places," Yohanan protested. "If you don't give them what they want, they might just kill you for sport. It happens every time Herod goes to his fortress palace at Masada."

Men of the village ran to and fro, hiding food and possessions. Although the Essene residents lived as humbly as monks and shared everything, they did not want to surrender any of their meager resources, especially not to the Romans."

"Clear the way!" a Roman guard call out.

"We're trapped," Phoebe whispered. "There is no way out!"

Yohanan held up his hand for silence. The doorway was too low for the horses, and the soldiers did not dismount. The heaving chests of the horses and the bare legs and kilts of the soldiers was all they could see.

We are doomed, thought Phoebe, staring at two sets of hooves pawing the ground and blocking their escape.

"Wine!" A messenger called to the soldiers. "We have found their wine," the Roman commander called out. The horses spun around and they were off to celebrate.

Yohanan waited until they were out of sight. "Now!" he commanded, motioning to his twelve companions.

Derek and Phoebe hoisted the poles to lift the jar with the Isaiah scroll, and followed Yohanan. Their path led westward along a boulder-lined brook, which was only like a trickle of water. There were enough willow bushes to keep them out of sight.

Phoebe was tiring and just about to ask for help when Yohanan decided to take a break. He found a place along the brook behind some willows where they could watch the disturbance below.

"Refresh yourselves," Yohanan directed as he sat down on a broad stone. The young men opened their pouches on their belts and took out figs, nuts, and bread to eat.

Yohanan produce a piece of honeycomb, which he broke into three sticky pieces and offered to his guests. "I share with you what I have," he said to Derek, Phoebe, and Yaldar.

Yaldar declined.

"This is honey. Very delicious!" Yohanan declared. When Derek and Phoebe looked puzzled, he showed them how to suck the honey from the comb. "It's good for you too."

"I want to tell you something," Yohanan leaned down and whispered. "All my life I have waited for the Anointed One, the Messiah. You see, before I was born, an angel appeared to my father and told him that he would have a son, which is me. I am the "voice in the wilderness" that was predicted by Isaiah. I am telling everybody to prepare for the Messiah. That's my job."

Yohanan produced dried grasshopper-like insects from his pouch. "These are called locusts. This, and honey, is all I ever eat," he stated rather matter-of-factly. He bit into the bug, leaving one leg sticking out of the corner of his mouth, and chomped away.

Phoebe squirmed and shook her head when he offered one to her.

Derek had a little more time to process the situation. He took the bug, smeared it with the honey, and tried not to chew too much before he swallowed it whole.

Yohanan nodded his approval and offered Derek another.

"Not too bad," Derek said with a grin. He took it from Yohanan, spread a little more honey on it, and popped it in into his mouth. For his sister's benefit, he made a slurping noise, licking the honey off of his fingers.

"Yuck," she protested.

"Now, where was I? Oh yeah, we knew that Messiah was born shortly after me, to Mary, who is my mother's cousin. There was even a great caravan that came from Persia to worship him. But we lost track of him after he was born in Bethlehem. I only knew his name, Yeshua."

Yohanan sat still for a bit. "I always knew I would recognize Messiah when I saw him. Yesterday it happened. I was at the Jordan River, preaching and baptizing. For years I have warned people to get ready."

"But I wasn't ready. Yeshua came to the river. He asked me to baptize Him. The Messiah asked to be baptized by the messenger! I told him it should be the other way around."

"When He came up out of the water, we all saw the skies open up and the Spirit of God descended on Him. At first we thought it was a white dove. You know, like Noah. We all heard the voice from heaven say, 'This is my beloved Son. Listen to Him.' Then Yeshua nodded to me, whispered, 'farewell, shalom,' and walked silently away into the desert wilderness, out of sight."

Suddenly, Yohanan stopped speaking. The soldiers down in the village had gotten back on their horses and were at the library.

"They have dismounted and gone inside where the remaining jars are. The only thing worse than a Roman soldier is a *drunken* Roman soldier," Yohanan muttered. "How long can our peaceful way of life withstand this oppression?" He stood silent as a statue, stunned by the sound of crashing pottery. Eventually the noise ceased.

Yohanan and his friends watched in horror as the soldiers came out of the library holding papyrus scrolls and pieces of parchment as trophies. Then they mounted up and headed south toward Masada.

"What was in those other jars?" Derek asked.

"Many of our stories and our records," Yohanan replied. "But the Romans have not destroyed everything. Today we saved the Books of Moses, the Prophets, and Poets. We also have saved many other writings and documents from our daily lives . . . and predictions about the coming war between light and dark. The Isaiah scroll you are carrying, for instance, contains predictions about our Messiah, the Anointed One . . ." He stopped speaking and looked at Derek and Phoebe.

How do they know? Derek thought.

"Elohim has kept it from falling into the hands of the Romans," Yohanan explained. "In the future these might be found, and our descendants will know about us."

"The time capsule would not be complete without Isaiah," Yaldar whispered to Derek and Phoebe.

As they were walking, Yohanan turned to Yaldar and said, "Traveler, something bothers me."

Yaldar furrowed his brow and tipped his head. "With all of this good news, how could anything be bothering you?"

"I was born to be a prophet," The Voice declared. "My father was a priest, and I began to study the holy scriptures while sitting at his knee. I have memorized the law and the prophets. The prophet Isaiah makes many predictions about the coming Messiah, who will reign with peace and justice. He will sit on the throne of David. He will be our king. He will heal the sick and set captives free. But who is he writing about when he says this?"

He was wounded for our transgressions,
He was bruised for our iniquities;
The chastisement for our peace was upon Him,
And by His stripes we are healed.
All we like sheep have gone astray;
We have turned, every one, to his own way;
And the Lord has laid on Him the sins of us all.

"Then, King David writes in the Psalms:"

My God, My God, why have you forsaken me . . .
The congregation of the wicked has enclosed Me.
They pierced My hands and My feet;
I can count all My bones.
They look and stare at Me.
They divide My garments among them,
And for My clothing they cast lots.

"Who is he talking about, if you know? When I encountered Yeshua, he did not act like the warrior I was expecting."

"In time you will know, my friend," Yaldar replied. "For now, just rejoice in the joy you found yesterday, and continue to cry out the message of Messiah's arrival."

One by one the jars were placed in the cave. Derek and Phoebe were careful to place the Isaiah scroll right where the Bedouin would find it, covered by the dust of time.

"We are returning another way," Yaldar said to Yohanan. "Go in peace."

As Yohanan and his friends descended the hill, Derek, Phoebe, and Yaldar watched silently.

Across the valleys were many limestone cliffs pocked with caves. "Other jars will be stored in some of those caves and will become part of the time capsule," Yaldar said.

"We need something for the weaver. Where is the blood in Qumran?" Phoebe asked.

"It's the Crimson Words that Yohanan quoted," Yaldar replied. "For now, perhaps that red flower blooming by the entrance of the cave will have to do."

"All caves are connected if you have the right tools," Yaldar grinned. He entered a cave and tapped his staff to the ground. The red dot appeared on the wall and immediately grew into the glowing oval portal that opened into Sophia's workshop.

18

CAPSULE

Present Time

Sophia was waiting with a plate of figs when the portal opened.

Phoebe stepped through first, extending her arm to present the red flower. "For you," she said.

"A wild red tulip from the desert," Sophia said with a warm smile. She examined its bright red petals. "It is so beautiful. Do you know how rare it is to find this flower? It doesn't bloom every year, only when the weather is perfect—and just in the springtime."

Sophia put it in a small clay vase and placed the blossom in the center of her table. Tea was ready, along with her usual hummus and cave flatbread and the few figs Derek had not yet polished off.

"Please, tell me about your journey," she said.

"It was a little confusing at first. We went to modern times, in 1947, and watched the Bedouins discover the Dead Sea Scrolls," There was a Haboob. Derek grinned, "Then, without going anywhere, we went back in time over two thousand years to the time of Jesus, or should I say Yeshua? Everything was exactly the same, except the dust on the jars. Nothing had happened in those caves for thousands of years. It was incredible!"

"We met the Essenes and John the Baptist," Phoebe continued. "What an amazing man. We helped them hide the scrolls in the caves. John told us how he baptized Yeshua and how he heard the voice of Elohim and saw the Spirit descend like a dove. He was so wound up."

"Wouldn't you be? So, what was in the jars?" Sophia asked.

"John said the Bible was in them, but since it was the day after Yeshua was baptized, it had to be just the Old Testament, right?"

"Right," Sophia agreed.

"When John quoted Isaiah and the Psalms, we were so surprised. It sounded just like he was talking about Jesus on the cross," Derek said.

"Those are the Crimson Words," Sophia said.

"Yes," Derek replied, "but it hadn't happened yet, right? They were just—"

"Predictions," Phoebe interrupted. "I get it."

"So, what did you bring to restore the Tapestry?" Sophia asked as she turned the Isaiah panel in her hands, examining the reverse, then the front. "This is almost impossible to make out. The color is completely gone, and the weaving is dilapidated."

"We looked for something with blood, but this flower is all we could find," Phoebe said.

"Thank you. It is beautiful, but it will not help to restore the Tapestry. Don't worry. Tomorrow you can retrieve another crimson thread," Sophia continued. She picked up another small section of the torn fabric over on the table. "This panel tells the story of the Battle of Jericho. Do you know it?"

"Yeah," Derek replied. "Joshua's army marched around Jericho. They blew the trumpets, 'an the walls came a tumblin' down,' right?"

"That is the song," she said.

Phoebe and Derek exchanged glances.

Sophia turned to address them face-to-face. "You will have no problem finding the crimson thread this time, but it might be difficult to retrieve."

19

RAHAB'S RESCUE

c. 1460 BC

*Y*aldar motioned for the kids to follow him. He took his usual few steps toward the back wall of the cave and tapped his staff to the ground. The red dot appeared. The shimmering rosy band expanded. Derek, Phoebe, and Yaldar stepped through the portal into an immense limestone cave lit by the golden glow of oil lamps.

"Whoa," Derek exclaimed, "this cave is huge. Just look at those carved pillars. They support the ceiling, don't they? That means this is a man-made cave."

"Right. In time it will be called Solomon's quarry," Yaldar stated.

"Makes sense. It's limestone," Derek observed. "That's what the temple was made of."

Sweaty stonecutters wearing only tattered linen kilts wielded bronze hammers and chisels in a deafening rhythm. The cave was cool with a musty smell accented by smoke from the burning oil lamps. As they walked out of the cave, the morning sun was just rising over the Jordanian hills.

"We are heading south toward Jericho," Yaldar said. "The Dead Sea is about twelve miles away."

Before long Phoebe spotted a man walking toward them. "What do you suppose he wants?" she questioned.

"Hard to tell," Yaldar replied.

"Just look at how he walks. He wants something," Phoebe insisted.

When the man got close enough, Yaldar called out to him, "Peace, friend. Shalom."

The man did not answer until he stood right in front of them.

Yaldar spread his hands, signaling for Phoebe and Derek to stand behind him.

The man was clearly a warrior of the desert. He wore a tan kilt, an open vest, and sandals. A rope belt supported his small pouch and a scabbard protecting a cubit-long sword with a white bone handle. His tan headscarf was made of a single piece of woven brown wool. The only thing about him that wasn't the color of desert were his eagle eyes. Light hazel in color, they were constantly scanning everything. He inspected Derek, then he studied Phoebe's face.

"Who are you, and why are you here?" he demanded.

"And you are?" Yaldar answered with a question.

"I am a guard of the camp of Israel. Why are you here?"

"I am Yaldar, friend of Joshua."

The man studied Yaldar's sandals, his robe, his staff, his un-desert-like hat, and then looked deep into his eyes.

"You know Joshua . . . from where?"

"Egypt."

"And you found us here?"

Yaldar nodded. "Please lead us to him."

The man pointed with his nose and started walking south. As they walked he spotted the thread around Phoebe's wrist. "What is the meaning of that?" he asked.

Phoebe paused, not knowing what she dared to divulge. "It's for our quest," she replied.

The man gave her a quizzical look. He began to warm up a little. "My name is Salmon," he said. Do you know what is happening today?"

Yaldar nodded again.

As they walked, a towering, walled city came into view.

"Jericho," Salmon said and pointed. The fortress city was protected by double walls with an earthen incline between them.

"Gotta be ten stories high," Derek whispered to Phoebe. "It looks impossible to scale those walls."

"We cannot defeat a city like this," Salmon said. "Not without a miracle. Of course, we are not strangers to miracles. I went there with my cousin Avner to spy out everything about the land and this city. We disguised ourselves with the armor we had captured from the Amorites.

"Just inside the gate a woman approached us. Her name is Rahab. She is beautiful. She has raven black hair. She wore gold earrings and her eyes are like pools of—" Salmon paused. "She invited us to her house above the city wall where she had been watching us from her window.

"Soldiers almost caught us. Around sunset, the king's soldiers came looking for us. Rahab took a huge risk. She had figured us out. 'You are not Amorites,' she'd said. 'I know Amorites. They are rough and disrespectful, especially the soldiers. I watched you analyze our gates. You are Hebrews. I am sure of it. The news of you travels fast. We have heard how your God is with you, and nobody can withstand you. Believe me, all of Jericho is afraid of you.'

"Before long we made a deal with her. Rahab hid us under a pile of flax that was drying on her roof. She lied to the king's soldiers, telling them that we were already gone, and they went out looking for us just before the city gates were closed. They did not find us, obviously. She told us about Jericho, its army, archers, and fortifications. In return, we promised to save her and her family . . . on one condition. We gave her a crimson cord to hang out her window. It is the signal that she and her family are the ones to be spared when we take this city. Then, she helped us get away."

❄ ❄ ❄

Salmon stopped and pointed to a burly man with wiry salt-and-pepper hair and a massive, graying beard. "There is Joshua," he said.

When Joshua saw Yaldar's brimmed hat, he recognized him immediately and motioned for him to come to his side. They embraced.

"Joshua, my friend, you remember Derek and Phoebe from Mt Sinai."

"Of course, and you are just as I remember you," Joshua said with a quizzical look on his face. "Time has been good to you," he said.

"Welcome. We are just about to take this city for the Lord. You have arrived at exactly the right time. Today we will begin to take the land promised by God to Abraham."

Then Joshua stepped onto a high rock. He raised his staff and waited for everyone to give him their attention. Then he addressed the people.

"For forty years I have dreamed of this moment. Forty years ago, with your parents, I followed Moses out of Egypt and out of slavery. We passed through the Red Sea on dry land. Forty years ago I spied out this land with Caleb.

"We do not fear this fortress. We do not fear the giants in this land. For forty years Elohim, the Almighty, has led us, fed us, and brought victory to our armies. You yourselves have crossed the Jordan River on dry ground.

"Now, in the name of The Lord, our God, we will prevail."

"Take up the ark!" He commanded.

The entire camp sprang into action. Seasoned soldiers formed a forward guard in front of the priests. Seven priests with shofar-trumpets made from ram's horns, took their place in front of the ark, but they did not make a sound.

The priests were very careful not to touch the ark. Poles ran through hoops on each side. When the priests lifted up the poles, the ark of the covenant could be seen above the heads of the people.

When the priests lifted the ark, Phoebe's heart skipped. *Finally, I will see it,* she thought. But no.

"It has to be covered by layers of fabric and skins when it is being moved. Remember, only the High Priest sees it." Yaldar explained. "Only the veil touches the ark, over that are ram skins dyed red, and the badger skins."

Bummer, thought Phoebe.

Silently the Israelites walked around Jericho as they had done for the previous six days.

Salmon whispered to Derek and Phoebe, "Watch for the crimson cord hanging from Rahab's window. It is near the main gate. We will go there and rescue her and her family."

Derek and Phoebe wound their headgear to cover their faces, protecting them from the sun and dust. Yaldar raised a scarf over his nose.

At last, the assembled Israelites began to move. Salmon made a circling motion, then held up five fingers on his right hand and two on his left.

Seven, he mouthed.

It took over an hour for the Israelite forces to walk around Jericho one time.

Derek did the calculation. "The city perimeter is about three miles," he observed. The last of the army was just starting to move by the time the ark completed its loop. And so, the city was encircled by the constant blaring of the shofar-trumpets followed by throngs of silent people. And all were led by the ark.

The city walls were lined with archers sizing up the Israelites. *We must look like ants to them*, Derek thought. *We are not out of range. They could kill us at any time.*

Salmon pointed to a window high on the city wall near the main gate, from which spilled a crimson cord dangling down the side of the wall.

Rahab, he mouthed.

Another hour. Another lap. He pointed again. *Crimson cord.*

The hot desert wind kicked up as they continued to circle the city.

Again. Phoebe rolled her eyes. *We've already done this twice. Can't we just—?*

Salmon seemed to read her mind. He held out five fingers on one hand to signify what was left.

Phoebe sighed and kept moving.

At the end of the seventh circuit, Joshua climbed up onto the rock again and raised his staff high into the air. Everything stopped. The trumpets stopped. Silence. The soldiers and the priests with the ark turned to face the main gate. Each of the Israelites faced the city wall.

Salmon pointed. Hanging out the window was the red cord, just beneath the archers lining the city walls. Derek imagined the shower of arrows they were about to pour down on them.

The bronze ornament on top of Joshua's staff reflected the sunlight.

"Now! The Lord has given us the city!" Joshua called out.

The ram's horn trumpets reverberated against the city walls.

The people ran forward, roaring a mighty battle cry.

Like a noose constricting its victim, the Israelites all ran straight ahead toward the city wall.

Suddenly, the ground started to rumble underfoot. The flight of arrows never came. The city walls began to collapse. Archers tumbled down and disappeared into the piles of rubble and dust.

Yaldar grasped the arms of Derek and Phoebe and drew them close so they could hear him say: "Get the crimson thread!" Then he released them to run to the city with Salmon.

When Derek and Phoebe reached the wall, Salmon was already standing over a pile of rubble. People were screaming, and fires began to burn throughout the city.

"Rahab! Rahab," Salmon cried out. "Where are you? You cannot be dead," he insisted to himself. "I gave my word we would save you. But now there is nothing here but a pile of bricks and stones. How could you survive?"

"Dig," Salmon commanded. He moved one brick and stopped. The whole pile of rubble shifted.

Derek remembered a program about Urban Search and Rescue. *Make sure when you move a brick or stone that it doesn't cause anything else to shift. It could crush them. Only move one brick at a time. Could anyone have survived the collapse?* he wondered. The search was frantic.

"The red cord. I see it!" Derek cried out.

Feverishly and carefully. Salmon, Avner, Derek, and Phoebe removed each brick as they followed the cord.

"Rahab!" Salmon called out.

"Rahab?"

"Here," Rahab coughed. "We are all here, and we are safe. Please get us out."

Stone by stone a passage was cleared. One by one, Rahab's family crawled out of the narrow tunnel in the rubble, welcomed by Salmon and Avner.

"Wait a minute," Phoebe cried out. Where is the cord? It was right here. I don't see it. We can't go back without it," she protested. "We will never get to our father."

Derek turned to Rahab. "Where is the other end tied off?" he demanded.

"Inside. It was tied to my bed."

Derek and Phoebe looked at each other.

"We have to get it," Phoebe said.

Using an army crawl, the pair scrambled through the precarious tunnel supported by the beams of Rahab's house. There was no light.

Finally, a glimmer from Yaldar's blue light flickered up the passageway. Together they found Rahab's bed with the cord still tied to it. In the rubble Derek found a sharp-edged stone. He cut a strand from the cord with it and tied it around Phoebe's wrist.

Immediately, Yaldar tapped his staff to the ground. The red dot expanded, but only enough to crawl out through. Phoebe went first, then Derek and Yaldar. The portal snapped closed while a loud rumble of falling bricks behind them.

The three of them stood up. They were in Sophia's workshop covered head to toe in dust.

Sophia emerged from the shadows. She started to embrace her new arrivals until she saw how dirty they were, then caught herself.

"Dust yourselves off," she directed. "We have work to do."

AFTER THE CRASH

Workshop

Sophia located the Jericho panel and gently placed it to the center of her table right in front of Phoebe.

"Take it," Sophia said.

Phoebe was still shaking from all of the crashing walls and their narrow escape, but she steadied herself and lifted the thread. In the panel she found what she thought should be Rahab's window near the gate. She moved the thread slowly across the surface until the thread touched the point where it belonged.

If a thread could dance, this would have been the time. Phoebe felt the vibration in her fingers. It was home. She released it and watched as the thread braided itself into the tapestry exactly where it had hung on the real wall of Jericho an hour ago. As it did, vivid color returned to the entire panel. The scarlet signal that had saved Rahab and her family was very easy to see, and it had saved part of the Tapestry.

With great satisfaction, Sophia turned to Derek and Phoebe. "This finishes the predictions. I am so proud of you."

Derek and Phoebe smiled.

Sitting at tea, Sophia cleared her throat. "Next," she said, "you must see how the predictions are fulfilled. "The night before Jesus was crucified, He ate the traditional Passover meal with His disciples. At that meal He instituted the Lord's Supper, which is known to many as the Eucharist or Holy Communion, and is celebrated by all Christians wherever they are in the world. After His Last Supper, He led his disciples to the Garden called Gethsemane, where He prayed and then surrendered Himself to the temple guard. Jesus was taken to a series of phony trials. First by the High Priest, then the Jewish Council, and then to King Herod."

"This very morning," Sophia explained, "Jesus has been taken back to the governor, whom Caesar had appointed to keep the region under Roman control: Pontius Pilate.

"You will need to bring back one more red thread, she explained. "This is the most important thread of all. Be very diligent. Be very alert to seize your moment and collect the thread."

Without a word, Yaldar faced the cave wall and tapped his staff to the ground. The dot was deep, dark red, and the perimeter was even darker. It wobbled only a little.

SACRIFICE

AD 33
Jerusalem

21

PASSOVER DAY

Daybreak

The portal closed. The darkness weighed on them. Derek ran his hand slowly along the wall. "This isn't an ordinary cave," he observed. "Maybe the walls have been plastered. It's hard to tell before the first light light, but I think I can see some artwork there."

Phoebe's hand swept across a smooth stone slab jutting out from the wall.

"They will lay him there," Yaldar said softly.

"Who?" she asked.

"Yeshua, of course."

"Then this is the . . ." she withdrew her hand and held it to her heart.

"This is the tomb of a very rich man," Yaldar explained. "His name is Joseph, from the town of Aramathea. Today he will ask Pontius Pilate to let him have Yeshua's body. Joseph will give Yeshua an honorable burial in his own tomb."

Not just another limestone cave, thought Derek.

Silently, Yaldar led the pair out of the tomb and into a large garden where they all turned around and faced the entrance.

"Look at that giant millstone!" Phoebe exclaimed. "Is that what they use to close the tomb?"

"Yes. That stone and over a dozen Roman soldiers, who will seal it and pledge to fight to the death to keep it sealed. At least, that's the plan." Yaldar winked.

Derek studied it. *The millstone is much bigger than the one in Dikuyu. I wonder if we find a clue how to move the wheel so we can get back to our dad? Doesn't look so easy.*

"This is going to be a hard day," Yaldar said. "We begin by going down to the center of Jerusalem. During Passover, Jews come here by ships, and by camel caravans, and most of them walk. Some come from thousands of miles away," Yaldar explained. "There are nearly a million people here right now, and the Roman army is in full riot-control mode. They don't want any trouble. Their horses and chariots are out to show everybody that Rome is in command here."

"This is way too quiet," Phoebe said. "The shops are all closed. It is not the same without the noise and aroma of nuts and meats roasting."

"Preparations for the Passover are mostly completed," Yaldar explained. "Everything has been cleaned and is free of any leaven, as they call it. Today they will kill the Passover lamb. One for each family."

"Just like in Egypt and on Mt. Sinai?" Phoebe asked.

"Yes, and every year from then to now," Yaldar replied.

"Hey, watch it!" Derek yelled when one of the mounted soldiers knocked him into a wall. "They don't seem to care about anybody," he said, dusting himself off. "All they care about is keeping themselves in power."

"That's right," Yaldar replied. "It doesn't matter to them who gets hurt in the process either. Kill or be killed; it's the way of the Empire." Soon they would arrive at the headquarters of the

Roman Army, which is also the Palace of the Governor, Pontius Pilate.

Yaldar picked up the pace. "Yeshua's trial is just beginning. We need to move," he said. The old man's stature and his distinctive hat made him very easy to follow. All along the way the people were buzzing about Yeshua.

"Last night He was arrested by the temple guards," Yaldar explained. "They threw Him in the high priest's dungeon. This morning He was interrogated by Pilate. Then they shuffled Him off to Herod, who couldn't find any charge that would stick, so now He is back here. Pilate is forced to make the decision."

"That sounds like the politicians are playing hot potato, trying to find anything that will convict Jesus," Derek observed.

"Some things don't change," Yaldar stopped and turned to Phoebe and Derek. "On our previous missions, we have gathered blood-red threads from the symbolic events. This will be different. Jesus is bleeding. Many predictions will be fulfilled today."

22

JUDGMENT

~∽~

Early Morning

"Bring me a basin of water," a gravelly voice bellowed from the balcony just as Yaldar and his two travelers arrived.

What is he so upset about? Phoebe wondered.

"I do not find any fault in this man," the voice continued.

A tall, steely eyed, clean-shaven man stood above them on the balcony. He wore a regal white toga. A sash with gold filigree was draped over his official tunic. On his right forefinger he wore a gold signet ring. The man was clearly important, and he was disgusted. He thrust his hands into the basin and then lifted them high so that the rowdy mob could see his washing motion. He scowled and then glanced at Yeshua, who looked back at him silently.

"That is Pontius Pilate," Yaldar said. "He rules this part of the Roman Empire. Only Caesar has more power . . . and Caesar isn't here."

"Crucify him," the accusers cried out.

"See to it yourselves," Pilate railed at the angry crowd. He dried his hands with a towel and angrily thrust it into the bowl.

"My soldiers will help you, but first I will have him scourged." He pivoted back into his palace, leaving the noisy mob behind.

"Pilate is trapped, isn't he?" Derek said. "He may have all of the power, but he can't release Jesus, not without risking some kind of revolt. Still, how can he pronounce anybody to be innocent and not set the person free?"

"Clear the way!" Heavy footsteps announced the arrival of the Roman enforcer. The mob parted as he strode across the stone courtyard and stared right at Yeshua.

The soldier was the epitome of manhood. *Buff*, thought Phoebe. His uniform presented him as a force of the Empire. The Roman kilt displayed his powerful legs. Leather straps around his calves held his thick sandals in place.

After he removed his brass helmet, Phoebe could see his clean-shaven face and neat jet-black hair. It was combed to the front and had no part. She studied his dark Mediterranean complexion and his large curved nose. A shiver went up her spine. She had felt it on more than one occasion, but never like this. There was a "presence." It was more than just the power of Rome. There was another force, and she felt it.

"Look at his eyes," she said to Derek. "Who does he remind you of?"

Derek studied the dark glare for a moment. "The serpent in the garden. They are like black fire."

"Yeah," agreed Phoebe. "Pure evil. He wants to kill and destroy. Just look at him. His heart is pounding, and his feet are pawing at the ground like a horse before the race."

"Or the battle," Derek added. "Just look at that whip. Have you ever seen anything like that? It is nothing like the cowboy whips we have in movies. It's got eight or nine strips of leather."

"That is a scourge," Yaldar said. "There are sharp pieces of metal and shards of bone and broken glass tied into each strip.

The Romans say that forty lashes will kill a man, so they will give Yeshua thirty-nine."

Phoebe's eyes widened. *No!* she mouthed.

"Strip Him!" barked the enforcer's gravelly voice.

Two other soldiers grabbed Yeshua's hands and raised them high, strapping Him to a stone pillar about eight feet tall. His body was stretched fully.

"Doesn't He know this is coming?" Phoebe whispered to Derek. "Can't He do something?"

The enforcer let the whips strands fall to the pavement and the metal and glass clattered ominously. The crowd grew silent as the enforcer bound His right hand to the handle of the scourge.

"That will give him more power," Yaldar whispered. "Pain is his specialty."

"And he clearly enjoys it," Derek observed.

The soldier took his stance, eyeing Yeshua's back like a pitcher surveying the strike zone.

With a single motion, the silence was broken. The torturer's arm reached high into the air. The whip jumped into action, its tentacles whistling as they rose to the attack. The pieces of metal and glass flashed in the morning light.

Phoebe winced.

Yeshua's body flinched. The shards penetrated. Then the tormentor began slowly drawing the whip across his victim's back, making sure to inflict as much pain as possible, yet Yeshua did not cry out.

"Stripes!" Phoebe's eyes widened.

"Stripes," she repeated as she stared at the red gashes.

"These are the—" She winced again as the whip dug deeper. "These are the stripes from the predictions: 'By his stripes we are healed.' When Yohanan quoted it at Qumran, I was confused. Now I see it."

Suddenly Phoebe doubled over and covered her mouth. Derek grabbed his sister, put his arm around her, and turned her away from the scene. Together they stood frozen as they listened to the slow tempo of the blows. She wanted to hurl but managed to hold it back. The full force of the Empire began to crush the One it had just declared to be innocent.

"Three, four." Time seemed to stand still as the scourging rhythmically persisted in the background. "Thirty-eight, thirty-nine," Derek counted. The tentacles clattered on the stone floor for the last time.

"Crucify him!" a voice broke the silence. "Crucify!" another called. "Crucify him!" the crowd intensified. The voices ricocheted off the stone walls of Pilate's palace.

Immediately, the Roman guards moved into riot control mode. At first, they surrounded Yeshua as if they were protecting Him. Then their mood changed. A guard called out, "Let's have some fun with 'im before we sends 'im up the mountain to His destiny."

"A king, is He?" another guard mocked. "I have just the thing for 'im. We made it special for today. Our King, Caesar in Rome, wears a crown woven from beautiful, soft leaves and flowers, but in this god-forsaken desert all I could find today is this." He cackled as he raised a crudely woven crown made from a local thorn bush. The spines were extremely long, stiff, and very sharp.

"And what else do we 'ave for the king?" he said, smirking. "Oh yes. A red robe. Put it on 'im. This is the day of your coronation, your highness." They laughed as the guard draped the robe on Yeshua's back.

He was blindfolded, and the crown of thorns was thrust on his head, forcing the spines like a flight of miniature spears into his skull. Blood gushed from each point of penetration. "Nothin' bleeds so well as the skull," the mockery continued. "If you are a prophet, tell us who hit you." The soldiers yelled as they hit him and spit on him.

Yeshua staggered and waited while two Roman soldiers removed the red robe. "He won't be needin' this anymore; put his old stuff back on 'im," the soldier sneered.

Derek and Phoebe watched Yeshua's tunic turn bright red as it soaked up his blood.

A large wooden crossbeam was then hoisted onto his bleeding back. Soldiers cleared the way through the surrounding mob. Slowly the swarm of people wound through the city gates and outside the city wall to the hill called Golgatha, meaning "the place of the skull."

Heartsick, Phoebe looked into the vapid eyes of one young soldier. *How could they do this like it was 'just a job'?*

As the crowds moved on, Phoebe and Derek scanned the court for something they could take to the weaver to restore the Tapestry. "There"—she pointed—"beside the whipping post." Together she and Derek hurried to examine a bloody shard of broken glass.

Before Derek could bend over to pick it up, he came face-to-face with the black eyes of the Roman enforcer, whose whip was still wound in his hand.

Derek started to panic. Instinctively, he backed away from the tormentor.

Phoebe! Derek positioned himself between the soldier and his sister, trying to prepare for the worst. Slowly, they backed away, keeping a close eye on the soldier. With the other eye, he searched for Yaldar but without success.

"Half the time they die right here," the enforcer mumbled as he shook his head and glanced at the whipping post, "but he's nothing like the others."

"Forget it," Derek groaned, leaving the glass shard lying at the tormentor's feet.

"Maybe we can get a thread from Jesus' robe," Derek said.

Phoebe felt like she was still choking. Her eyes were reddened, and her emotions were frazzled. The air was dark with clouds and heavy with smoke from the nearby temple where the priests were preparing for the Passover feast.

Derek watched her and tried to steady her. "You Okay?" he asked. He knew she wasn't.

Slowly she began to catch her breath and regain her composure. Then suddenly she was back, and with more determination than ever.

"We are on a mission here. Everything is at stake. We need to get a thread from Yeshua's robe, restore the Tapestry, then we can get back to Dad. Hurry up!" she said. "We have to get close to Jesus." Derek was stunned by the quick return of the old Phoebe. She plunged into the teeming crowd with renewed fervor, and she was small enough to slip through the gaps. That left Derek to push and shove his way through the angry mob.

The jeers of the throng were enough to make anybody sick. "Crucify him!" Over and over they repeated their mantra. "Crucify!"

Derek and Phoebe watched as the lynch mob grew. Confused spectators were drawn in. Soon others came behind and pressed them deeper into the crowd. No longer on the fringes, many people just gave themselves over to the mob spirit.

Phoebe shuddered as the cries got louder.

Yeshua's followers were there, too, but they kept their distance. They were horrified and afraid. *If this could happen to their leader, what would happen to them?* Phoebe pondered. They hid, but still they had to see.

Some were weeping uncontrollably. "This just can't really be happening," Derek heard a voice in the crowd say. "We were so sure He would make everything right."

"Now, they will kill us too," Phoebe heard, "just for following Him."

"He has fallen." The message rippled through the onlookers. Although the crowd had stopped, Phoebe had not. Her elbows continued to fly as she pressed closer to where Jesus was.

The Roman guards kept everyone at bay— except Phoebe. She popped through the line of soldiers and suddenly was face-to-face with Yeshua. She barely recognized Him. Rivulets of blood streamed down his face as if He had been engraved by dozens of thorn-tipped pens.

Impulsively, she grabbed her sleeve to mop Jesus' brow. Just when her hand was about to touch His face, a soldier pitched her back into the crowd.

When Derek finally reached her, she was shaking. "I almost touched Him," she said, sobbing. "At first I didn't recognize Him at all. He is so bloody and beaten, I couldn't really be sure was Him—except for His eyes. I will never forget His gaze. I felt love. I still feel His love."

Abruptly, one of the soldiers picked out a large man in the throng. "You! Carry his cross!" he commanded.

"It's Simon from Africa," a bystander said, identifying the powerful man who towered over most of the crowd. His bright white tunic accentuated the elegance of his dark skin. Reverently, he hoisted the beam off Yeshua's back and took it on his own shoulder. Simon stood still and offered his hand to Yeshua, who took hold and slowly rose to his feet, stabilizing Himself by holding onto Simon for a brief distance.

"That's enough," the soldier barked. Simon gently set the beam on Yeshua's shoulder, trying to help Him find an easier position.

"Maybe it did help," Derek muttered as he watched Yeshua draw strength from the brief assistance and genuine kindness. He thought Phoebe was listening, but when he looked, she had disappeared again.

23

CRUCIFIXION

c. 9 AM – 3 PM

What a chaotic place, Derek thought. He shuddered as he arrived at the top of the hill and stood among the crowd, waiting for Yeshua to finish His climb. *Yaldar is still nowhere to be found, and now I have lost Phoebe.*

"Phoebe?" He called out, but at a cautious volume. How could he pick her out of the crowd? She wore a long tunic and a headscarf of brown and gray like most of the women. Instinctively, he looked down for her blue-and-white sneakers until he caught himself. *Guess not,* he sighed, *she has sandals too.*

Don't panic, Derek told himself, but it wasn't working. He was freaking out. *What am I doing here? First, we lost our dad. Then we trusted Yaldar, and he has disappeared. Now I have lost my sister. I'm completely alone and abandoned in this barren, god-forsaken place and time. People are filled with hatred and rage. If I die now, nobody will even notice.*

He could see members of the ruling class standing at a distance. They all wanted to be sure Yeshua was dead before the Passover feast began at sundown, but they did not want this man's blood on their hands. They wanted the Romans to do it.

Derek recognized some of the people who had been at Pilate's palace, calling for crucifixion. Pharisees and Sadducees, scribes and priests; all were identified by their rich clothing and refined demeanor. Each group had a different reason, but they agreed on one thing: getting rid of Yeshua—permanently.

The Romans were visible everywhere. They were hell-bent to see that the job was done quickly and right. "Pilate doesn't want any loose ends," the Centurion barked to his soldiers. "This Yeshua thing will be over by sundown tonight! Understand?" It was very clear; the Romans were in control.

Derek peered into the shadows. Mary, Yeshua's mother, was there with few other women who had followed Him, too, as well as John. Conspicuously absent were the other disciples.

Phoebe must be here somewhere, he reasoned.

Yeshua fell to the ground, dropping the beam. A foreboding *thud* echoed like a giant tree cut down at the hands of a logger.

Two criminals there were already hanging on crosses near the top of the hill. "Who are these guys? What did they do?" Derek muttered to nobody in particular.

"Thieves," a soldier responded. "We nailed 'em up earlier this morning. Bad guys." Then he added, "Some of 'em last for days up there, but they ain't seen the floggin' like this guy. Anyways, we got strict orders to get this all over today. We'll break his legs if we have to, then he'll die real fast."

Derek trembled as he watched one of the soldiers pick up a nail and turn it slowly in his hand. He showed no emotion when he ran his finger over the tip to check its sharpness.

One scraggly soldier walked up and kicked Yeshua, who was still lying beside the cross. "I heard about this one," he said. He glanced at the large crowd. "Usually nobody comes here to watch. I never seen so many . . . And big shots too."

Amid the cacophony and frenzy of the crowd, a scrappy soldier picked up the three signs sent by Pilate. "Looky 'ere," he chuckled. "Lotta guys gets a sign on top o' their cross sayin' what they done wrong. He gets three of 'em sent from Pont-tee-yus Pie-lut hisself. We always put right here above their head. What's it say? I can't read."

"King of the Jews," a voice called from the mob. "They're all the same. Just in Roman, Greek, and Hebrew."

"He don't look like no king now, does He?" the soldier cackled.

"Shut up and get on with it," the Centurion's voice rang out.

Immediately, the crucifixion routine sprang into action. First, they stripped him of all of His clothing. Then one soldier grabbed Yeshua's right hand, and another His left. They savagely jerked His body into position, flopping Him on top of the cross as it lay flat on the ground.

Points of the iron spikes were pressed into His hands. *Clang!* Heavy hammers came down like they were driving railroad spikes. Yeshua writhed in silent agony as the nails penetrated through His flesh and into the wood.

A small block of wood supported the bottoms of Yeshua's feet. *Clang!* The innocent Yeshua could now raise his body up to catch a breath.

Without missing a beat, the soldiers tilted the cross up with Jesus on it. When it was nearly vertical, gravity took hold and it dropped into a hole drilled long ago for this very purpose. *Thud!* The cross dropped nearly three feet. Then Yeshua's body was jolted to a halt by three spikes.

Derek shuddered when he heard Yeshua's bones popping out of joint.

"Phoebe," Derek whispered to himself. "Where are you? Don't look."

He watched Yeshua writhe trying to find relief from the excruciating pain. Yet Yeshua did not cry out.

For some time now, a profound darkness settled on the mountain. It lasted longer and was darker than a total eclipse. With it came the eerie, spine-tingling sense of the presence of evil.

Derek looked at Mary. *Is there any comfort for a mother who watches her son bear such injustice? This is totally evil. For Yeshua there is no relief, no escape, no dignity. He will die . . . soon.*

Derek heard bystanders mocking Jesus. "He saved others, let Him save himself," they cried.

Shut! Up! Derek thought.

The thief on one side of Yeshua challenged Him. "If you are the Son of God, save yourself and get us all out of here."

"I want the tunic," a soldier shouted. He scratched out a game in the dirt at the foot of the cross. Some soldiers picked up Yeshua's sandals and other garments, then sat down with small stones and gambled for the tunic—just passing the time.

Phoebe? Derek whispered. "Where are you? We still have to get a thread."

When he saw Yeshua's blood-drenched tunic lying nearby on the ground, he moved closer, trying not to be noticed. "Get away!" a soldier sneered, grabbing the tunic. "This is fer us! He sat on the garment and casually resumed the game.

Derek continued the search for his sister. "Phoebe?" he called. His eyes darted nervously. He wandered through the crowd, keeping his head low to avoid being recognized. Still, Phoebe was impossible to pick out.

He gazed back at Mary. *She is so small,* he thought. *Yet she is a giant to us.*

The smoke from the nearby temple was confined by the lowering clouds. It was as if the skies themselves were mourning.

Silence descended on the mountain. *I can feel the silence with my whole body*, Derek thought. *My senses are scrambled.*

When Derek looked back to Mary. He spotted his sister and began to walk toward her.

Phoebe's heart jumped when she saw her brother. She wanted to run to him but couldn't leave. Silently, she turned to Mary, took her hand, and gazed mournfully into her teary eyes. There were no words.

When she reached her brother, Phoebe buried her face into his shoulder. "When are they going to stop?"

"Not until *He* says, 'It is finished,' " Derek whispered.

Slowly, Yeshua straightened his legs and hoisted himself, gasping for air and transferring the agony from his arms to his feet.

He looked at the rulers and to the Romans and said, "Father, forgive them, for they know not what they do." Then He exhaled and sank for a time into silence.

Time passed.

Again, Yeshua lifted Himself and looked at John standing with Mary. "This is your mother now," He said, "take care of her." Then He said to his mother, "This is your son." It was such a compassionate moment in the middle of an eternal conflict.

"Do you remember the Passover in Egypt?" Derek asked.

Phoebe nodded.

"There were ten plagues, right? I never figured out the ninth plague. Do you remember what it was?"

Phoebe shook her head. "No."

"Darkness. It came just before the death of the firstborn sons."

"My God, My God, Why have you forsaken me," Yeshua cried out.

"That is from the predictions," Phoebe remembered. "In the Psalms."

One last time Yeshua straightened His legs, raised Himself, drew a large breath, and cried out in a loud voice, "It . . . is . . . finished!"

For the last time, He exhaled, then His weight settled on three nails.

"I can't stand it," whispered Phoebe."

In that moment all of Jerusalem felt a shaking. "Earthquake!" they screamed.

Derek watched as a elegantly-dressed member of the High Council left the mountain. Before long, the same man returned with a contingent of Pilate's guards. The man was tall and strode with confidence. Everybody could see by his robes, jewelry, and ornamented turban that he was wealthy and powerful.

"He wants Yeshua's body, to bury it," the Roman officer announced. "Pilate says he can have it."

"No way!" Protests rippled through the onlookers.

"A proper burial?"

"Out of the question!"

"Preposterous."

"He's a blasphemer."

"A criminal doesn't deserve respect."

"Why would Pilate even allow this? We did not agree to it!"

Amid the raging voices of the protests, they heard the familiar, calm voice of Yaldar say, "Don't be afraid."

When Phoebe turned to face him, she wanted to give him a piece of her mind. Instead, she flashed look of exasperation and almost instinctively hugged him.

"That is Joseph from Aramathea," Yaldar stated. "He will bury Jesus in his own tomb; the one you saw this morning. The leaders preferred the body be thrown into the garbage fires of the Hinnom Valley like a common criminal; not laid to rest in a rich man's tomb."

Wow, Derek pondered. *It would take a lot of guts to walk up to the most powerful man in this part of the Empire—someone who is already in a very bad mood—ask for Jesus' body . . . and get it.*

"Joseph has lost many friends today," Yaldar observed.

24

VEIL

~~~

Before Sundown

erek and Phoebe stood motionless with the rest of the onlookers as a soldier pierced the side of Jesus' lifeless body. Blood, and a clear liquid like water, flowed from the gash.

"As if crucifixion wasn't enough," Phoebe said, shuddering.

"Time to go," Yaldar remarked.

"But we didn't get a thread," Phoebe protested. "That was our last chance. We will never get back to our dad."

"We are not through," Yaldar replied.

Without a word, Derek and Phoebe followed Yaldar down the narrow streets and now-quiet passageways into the heart of Jerusalem. They passed through a dark stone archway when they felt their clothing transforming once again. Reemerging into the light, they studied their peculiar and ornate attire.

"What is this?" Derek asked.

"You are priests," Yaldar responded.

"That can't happen," Phoebe protested.

"It's different now," Yaldar replied.

Phoebe felt her turban and the cloth that draped behind her head conveniently concealing her hair. Derek wore the same impressively woven linen clothing. Over their white robes was a single, ornate blue fabric draped over them, front and back, and gathered at the waist by a woven belt. Their leather sandals were of excellent quality, and all the way around they looked regal. To their surprise, Yaldar also had a similar garment, but with more gold and silver on the sleeves and tassels at the hem.

"What's this for?" Phoebe was puzzled.

"Admission," Yaldar replied as he led them through the court of the Gentiles and up the steps of the temple. Priests, who dressed just like them, were scrambling everywhere and appeared to be in some kind of controlled panic mode.

"What's going on, Yaldar?" Derek questioned. "This place is a madhouse. Nobody even notices us. Are you sure we are okay?"

"They have a big problem," Yaldar said with a wink. He led them through the court of the Gentiles. Silently, they followed him right into the temple courtyard.

"Wow! This is just like what Bez showed us in the tabernacle, only giant sized!" Derek exclaimed. "There is the brass altar where they burned the offerings. The washing basin. It's like what we saw at Mt. Sinai, only huge. This is cool. Instead of a woven curtain, there are those massive brass doors guarding the Holy Place."

When Yaldar started to go in, Derek stopped him, grabbing his robe. "Where are you going, Yaldar? What is going to happen to us?

"Everything has changed," Yaldar replied.

"Do we need rope around our ankle? We have come too far. I don't want to die. I remember what Bez told us," Phoebe said, worry in her voice.

Yaldar paused. "Do you remember what happened at the moment after Jesus said, 'It is finished?' "

"He died," Phoebe said, matter-of-factly.

Yaldar wrinkled his face. "And?"

"And there was an earthquake," Phoebe recalled.

"That's right, Phoebe," Yaldar said. "And that shaking was *cosmic*. At the same time, something very symbolic happened inside this temple. As a result, the Holy of Holies is open to all who believe. Messiah Yeshua has opened up the way for us."

"What is the meaning of that?" Phoebe asked.

"What is this day in history?" Yaldar asked?

"It's Passover of course," Phoebe replied.

"Right, and He is the Passover Lamb of God, sacrificed for us. Let us now enter silently and with great reverence." Yaldar led them inside the Holy Place, which was lighted only by the golden menorah. They waited for their eyes to adjust.

Phoebe's nose twitched. "That's the incense I smell, isn't it?" she asked. "I like the aroma of it."

"Follow me. Walk slowly, and respect the Almighty," Yaldar instructed in a very low voice. "Do you remember what Bez said about the veil?"

"Didn't he say it was the place where Elohim spoke with Moses? Moses would be on this side of the veil, and Yahweh on the other."

"Look up," Yaldar directed. The veil was about twenty feet wide and suspended about sixty feet above them. It was about four inches thick with ornate embroidery.

"It's been torn all the way down," Phoebe whispered.

"What happened? What could possibly tear anything that thick?" Derek asked.

"The earthquake," whispered Phoebe.

"Maybe," Yaldar said, nodding, "but see, it was torn from top to bottom."

Derek and Phoebe stood transfixed beside the giant veil, admiring the ornate cherub-angels and other embroideries. The frayed strands waved in the gentle breeze.

Soon their eyes adjusted to the darkness, revealing the only object in the Holy of Holies.

"The ark!" Phoebe gasped, peering through the torn veil. "There it is! Right in front of us, with its solid gold crown around the top and the two solid gold cherub-angels. Look how their wings touching in the middle. It's just like Bez described it."

Phoebe grabbed her brother's hand and they stood speechless. An unseen force seemed to draw them toward the ark, and together they took one step inside the Holy of Holies; one step beyond the veil.

Just then a breeze stirred. A single thread came loose. It drifted from the very top of the curtain. It floated randomly, moving about on an ever-so-slight air current.

That's it! he thought. *We didn't get a thread from the scourging or the cross. I have to get it.* He had been so transfixed by the ark that he was afraid to move a muscle. *Please God.* Then, just as it was about to float into his hand, the breeze caught it again and lifted it above his reach. *I have to get it!* Derek was afraid to make any quick movements. *It has to be red.* He held both hands into the air and prayed. "Please, God," he whispered.

"Please, God," Phoebe echoed, lifting her hands up too.

The thread finally fluttered within Derek's reach. He stood motionless until it touched his fingertips. Surprisingly, it was heavy, not like any of the other threads they had recovered.

"Feel this," he said, handing it to his sister.

Phoebe gazed at it for the longest time, then reached out to take it. "It is heavy, she agreed. She felt it swirl around and snug itself onto her wrist.

"Ooh," whispered Phoebe. "I feel warm and wonderful all over. It is just like the feeling I had in the Garden of Eden before the fruit incident. Peace. Joy. No fear." She smiled, recalling the memory.

25

THE LAST RED THREAD

"Now we can go," Yaldar announced.

Suddenly one of the Temple priests, who was repairing the torn veil, spotted them inside the Holy of Holies. "You cannot be here!" he declared. "Actually, you should be dead." He shook his head. "What's going on here?"

Yaldar tipped his head to the surprised priest and led Derek and Phoebe right past him and out of the holiest part of the temple.

Each object took on new meaning as they passed it on their way. In a vacant corner of the Court of the Gentiles, Yaldar tapped his staff to the ground. The red dot appeared on a wall, and the wobbly oval grew into the brightest red yet and seemed to make a sound like soft reeds in the wind.

"Welcome back," Sophia said, rising from her loom to greet them. "Are you okay? Your faces look different."

"Are we okay? We have just seen Jesus get scourged, then crucified, and we saw the ark . . . and we are alive to tell about it." Slowly, Derek lifted his eyes to meet Sophia's. "I think I'm okay, but I will never be the same."

Phoebe nodded her silent agreement. "But we didn't get anything with Jesus' blood on it," she said. "We failed. What is going to happen now?"

"You did not fail, my dears," she said. "Let me see your wrist." Sophia reached out and gently retrieved the crimson thread from Phoebe's extended arm.

Joyfully she lifted it up and down to feel the weight of the thread.

"I will use this thread from the veil to restore the tapestry of the crucifixion."

"So we're done?" Derek suggested.

"Almost."

Phoebe raised an eyebrow.

"This story does not end at the cross. If that were true, it would be a sad story indeed. There is one more place you must visit. Yaldar will take you now, and I will see you very soon," Sophia said.

When Phoebe started to protest, Yaldar tapped the floor of the workshop. The red dot appeared, and the portal expanded.

REVELATION

26

EMMAUS

◦◦◦◦◦◦

Three Days Later

"Oooh, this looks like the Carlsbad Caverns." Phoebe's head whirled as she stepped through the portal. "Are we in New Mexico?"

"No," Yaldar chuckled. "This is the Emmaus Cave. We are only about seven miles from Jerusalem."

"These rock formations are awesome!" she exclaimed. "That one looks like Sophia. It is kind of shaped like her. And that one looks a little you with your hat, Yaldar. How do they get that way?"

"Water from the nearby Emmaus Hot Springs drips from the ceiling. When the water evaporates, tiny amounts of minerals build up over eons of time. Those that are like icicles hanging from the ceiling are called stalactites, and the ones that rise from the floor are called stalagmites," Yaldar said.

"Good to know," said Derek.

"It's beautiful," Phoebe gushed. "Maybe one of the most amazing things I've seen. But aren't we on a mission here? Our dad needs us. We need to get back to him."

"Yes, yes, my travelers. Follow me," said Yaldar as he led them out of the cave and joined the flow of pilgrims making their journey home from Jerusalem in the fading afternoon sunlight.

A small village of stone and brick construction lay directly ahead.

"This is Emmaus," Yaldar said. "In English you say 'Ee-may-yus,' but here they pronounce it like 'Ay-mouse.' "

"Is that in the Bible?" she questioned.

"It's in there."

Yaldar looked directly into the eyes of his young companions. "Your mission is slightly different this time. Three days have passed since we witnessed Jesus' crucifixion."

He waited.

"Then it's Easter!" Phoebe exclaimed. "It's the very first Easter. Jesus has risen today! This is the best day of all time!" Then she stopped and looked around. "This isn't right. Everybody seems to be scared and depressed."

"That's because we are among the very few who know . . . yet," Yaldar explained. "You have to remember, there is no 'electronic news feed' here. News travels on foot."

The sun was just setting. The line of worshippers returning from Passover turned to a trickle. "In order to complete your mission, there is one more person you need to meet. He will arrive soon."

Drawing near to a small dwelling, they heard a ruckus going on inside. "He's dead! Yeshua is dead," a man's voice shouted. "I *saw* him die. Right up to the end we believed. We watched from a distance. We were sure he would just get off the cross, or angels would rescue him or something. But no! He just hung there, cried out "it is finished," and died. We saw the Romans stick a spear into His side. Nothing could happen after that, so we left. We were so certain that He was Messiah. He was supposed to lead us. He was supposed to overthrow the Romans, but instead it's like He just stirred up a hornet's nest."

Passing chariots clattered along the stone street, drowning out the tirade. A woman's voice shouted back. "The Romans like to remind us that they are still in charge."

"Clearly, Yeshua was not Messiah after all." The man was furious at Jesus—almost totally unhinged. "He performed miracles and healed so many people, but in the end He couldn't save himself. No! It was all some kind of cruel hoax. I was a fool to believe."

"Stop that yelling, Avi!" the woman commanded. She sounded increasingly frustrated. "Where is your father and your uncle? Supper is ready! They should have been here hours ago."

A soft tap came at the door.

"Finally. They're back." The woman was relieved.

When she opened the door, she stepped backward and looked more than a little shocked. Instead of her husband and brother-in-law, she was looking up at Yaldar, with Derek and Phoebe standing beside him. *And right at supper time too*, she thought.

"Hello, Miriam," Yaldar greeted. She was not ready for visitors, but what could she do? She recognized Yaldar but could not really recall any specifics. "These are my companions, Derek and Phoebe."

"Foreigners, are they?" she muttered grudgingly as she swung the door open. "Welcome."

Yaldar and Derek had to duck through the low doorway into a tiny adobe brick structure. Miriam greeted them with a peck on the cheek that lacked sincerity.

Her servant washed the feet of the three while Miriam stared up the road, trying to pick out her husband, Cleopas, and his brother.

"Where are they?" she grumbled, trying to decide what to feed her surprise dinnertime arrivals.

"I think she feels embarrassed," Phoebe whispered to Yaldar. "It's dinnertime, and she has to feed her guests, invited or not. Obviously she is unprepared."

"Quickly," Phoebe heard Miriam say to her servant. "We need more food. Go next door and ask Sarah to lend us three loaves of bread. Also ask for hummus and cheese, as much as she will give. We must have enough."

Inside the house the angry voice ranted on. "Yeshua stood up to Herod. He stood up to the Temple priests! He stood up to Pilate and the whole Roman Empire! So what? Our hopes are all dead. Because *he* is dead!"

"Avi is so angry at Yeshua." Miriam apologized for her son. Then she lowered her voice. "Actually, we all are."

"Here they come," Avi announced, stopping his rant. "And there is someone else with them."

"That's just fine," muttered Miriam. "They will invite him to stay for dinner, I know it. Just one more mouth to feed."

The stranger stopped outside the house. He was clearly a man of tradition. He wore a shawl that covered his head and obscured his face. It was white with blue bands, and had the usual knots and tassels at the corners. It did not suggest that he was either wealthy or poor. His robe was long, revealing only the edges of his sandals as he walked.

Miriam was relieved when he started to go on down the road, then her husband called to him.

"Stay, friend." After a few moments the stranger nodded and turned toward the cottage.

"They killed Him, didn't they?" Miriam said to her husband softly before the stranger came within earshot. "We heard yesterday."

"Yes, they crucified Him, like a criminal. No respect at all. I couldn't bear to watch. But I couldn't look away either. He suffered for hours."

"Friend." Cleopas gestured as the stranger reached the door. "Please, come in. I want my family to meet you and to hear what you said about Yeshua and Messiah."

Miriam took her husband aside. She was fuming. "What took you so long? Your supper has been ready for hours. The bread has cooled. Now, because of this stranger and those kids, I have sent the servants to borrow more bread and cheese."

Yaldar observed that there was no one left to wash the feet of the stranger and gestured to Derek and Phoebe. She picked up a small earthen bowl and Derek poured water into it. The room grew very quiet. Phoebe wanted to say something, but frankly, she was afraid of Miriam. *And so*, she thought, *were the men.*

In the background she heard Cleopas explaining the events of the day to his wife. "The whole way from Jerusalem this stranger has walked with us. Funny, he never said his name. He said that this morning some of the women had gone to the tomb and came back claiming they had seen Yeshua alive. And this stranger believes it.

"I told him that we believed the true Messiah would be a conqueror, one who would never die. Therefore Yeshua could not have been Messiah. You have to hear him. He told us how it was possible. He started with Moses and explained the ancient scriptures like it had some kind of hidden message. He showed us that Messiah had to suffer. He showed us where it was all predicted and how Yeshua was the fulfillment of predictions nobody knew were even there."

Meanwhile, Derek and Phoebe had knelt down in front of the stranger and reached out to push the fringe of His robe aside so that they could wash His feet.

"Scars!" Phoebe mouthed.

Derek and Phoebe both froze when they saw each foot with a round white scar.

"I can't do it," Derek gasped. "I can't touch His feet. What will happen to me? How could these feet belong to the same man we saw hanging on the cross three days ago?"

When Derek slowly lifted his gaze upward until he could see the stranger looking back at him. The shawl covered His head, and it seemed like a tunnel with Derek and Phoebe on one end, and the Savior on the other, with nothing between.

The stranger nodded.

Derek was shaking. "I can't do this," he said.

Then they looked into the luminous eyes of the risen Jesus. A sense of peace engulfed them both.

Jesus nodded again as if to say. "Touch them; it is really me."

Phoebe touched Him first. Painful memories flashed through her mind and vanished.

Carefully, Derek touched the other scar. He washed and dried the Savior's feet. At first, they were afraid to touch Him, and now they were too awestruck to let go.

"I felt something," he whispered. "All of the places we have been on this mission swirled through my mind. I saw shadows of Yeshua in every scene."

"Do you smell that fragrance?" Phoebe whispered. "Four days ago, a woman poured a very expensive bottle of perfume on the feet of Jesus." She leaned closer and gently inhaled. "I think I can still smell it."

A slight breeze stirred a pure white silk strand that dangled from the corner of the stranger's shawl.

Derek glanced at Phoebe. "There is no red cord this time," she whispered.

"Yaldar said we would know."

Of course, he thought. *We heard Yeshua say 'It is finished.' No more red. No more blood. The sacrifice is complete.*

Derek touched the dangling strand. It was firmly attached. "How do you take it? You don't just cut something off of Jesus' robe."

Jesus looked at each one of them directly in the eye, then nodded. The strand slackened into Derek's hand. He handed it to Phoebe, and they watched it wrap around her wrist. *Mission accomplished*, he thought.

Just then, Miriam announced that dinner was ready and everybody should move toward the table.

The stranger sat in the place of honor.

"Blessed are you Lord God, King of the Universe," He began. It was the traditional blessing. Then he lifted the bread. His hands extended beyond his sleeves, and when He rotated them to break the bread, there was a collective gasp. They all saw the round white scars. Speechless, they watched as the stranger just disappeared.

Gone.

No one spoke for several minutes, after which Yaldar rose to his feet and bowed to the family. "Thank you, and peace," Yaldar said. "We must go now."

Without a word, Phoebe and Derek followed Yaldar back into the Emmaus cave.

The perimeter of the oval portal was now snow-white and seemed to give off its own light.

Sophia greeted them expectantly. Ecstasy broke across her wrinkled face as she gazed at the shining white strand.

"Now can we see our father?" Phoebe asked.

RESTORATION

27

TAPESTRY

Workshop

Tears of joy welled up in Sophia. Slowly she reached out, cupped Phoebe's face, and gazed deeply into her hazel eyes. She gently kissed each cheek. Then she turned to Derek and did the same thing, reaching up to draw his face close to hers. Well done, my son," she whispered.

She was almost shaking when she took Phoebe's hand. Then she gripped Derek's hand and led them to her worktable.

"Great art always requires the best materials," she said.

The Tapestry lay face down. It was easy to see that all of the pieces were oriented together like the back of a jigsaw puzzle. Each panel had been carefully woven into the triumphant work of art. The borders were clear, and much of the color was in place.

Sophia, together with Derek's and Phoebe's guiding the white strand to the lower right corner of the Tapestry. "Let there be light," she said.

A shiver went through Derek and Phoebe as the white silk strand began weaving itself through the pieces.

"It's not long enough," Derek said.

"There is plenty," Sophia whispered.

With nothing to do but watch, Derek and Phoebe held on to the edges as life returned to the fabric.

Without a word, Phoebe and Derek turned the Tapestry over.

"Bright red is in every panel," Yaldar said. "It is the thread of redemption and sacrifice. At the very top, above all of the panels, is the white panel of the risen Christ floating in midair. That is the way He left the earth . . . and the way He will return on that day." Suddenly the ground started to vibrate. The lamps began to flicker and go out as dust fell from the ceiling. Derek and Phoebe dove under the table until the earthquake ended and the dust settled.

28
HOME

~

Present Time

"Valdar, where is your light?" Phoebe called out.

No answer.

"Sophia? Are you here?" Derek inquired.

.

Suddenly they heard a voice.

"Phoebe? Derek?"

"Dad!" Phoebe was ecstatic.

"Are you okay?"

"Over here!" Derek yelled back.

Narrow beams from Borodin's flashlight sliced through the dusty air. Father and kids rushed toward each other, embracing in a long, tight, and teary-eyed family hug. "Let's get you out of here," Dr. Paloma insisted. "We need to call Mom. She has been freaking out. We've been searching for you for hours."

"Seemed a little longer to us," Derek replied.

Between hugs, Dr. Paloma held his kids at arms-length in order to check them out. He spotted the blood on Derek's pant leg.

"It'll wash out," Derek said. "Nothing serious."

"You look different. Were you scared?"

They exchanged glances.

"At times," Derek answered.

"Let's go call your mom."

Borodin and his team were on their phones talking to the other searchers. "They are safe," he reported. "We will bring them out immediately."

"Follow me," Borodin directed.

Phoebe reached out and caught her father's arm and stopped him. Something was very different about her insistent manner.

Derek surprised Borodin, by grabbing his flashlight. Scanning the room, he found Sophia's worktable and led the others to it. The Tapestry responded as they approached. Each panel revealed its story. Scenes appeared to be animated. Trees seemed to sway and the water gave the sense of motion.

"The Tapestry?" Dr. Paloma's eyes widened. "It wasn't just a story." Slowly he reached out and touched the fabric. He ran his hand across it, sensing its textures of wool, linen, and silk. "Each panel feels very different," he said. "It responds to my touch. I've never seen a more perfect artifact. Just look at the condition of this. When the people in Istanbul talked about a tapestry, I imagined something colorless and lifeless. You know, like other stuff we found around the world that took years to restore and many thousands of dollars. As soon as we get to Istanbul, will take this to Mrs. Kreesh at the Museum of Antiquities."

Derek handed the light to his father. Then he and Phoebe gently lifted the Tapestry up and turned it so Dr. Paloma could feel it.

"Do you remember Grandma Phebe telling us about a special tapestry hidden in a cave long before they came to America?" Phoebe asked.

"I always thought it was just a fairy tale. You know, 'once upon a time' stuff," Dr. Paloma replied. "This is impeccable! Unbelievable!" he said.

"It draws you in. Like it wants to take you to these places." Makes you feel like you're really there, doesn't it?"

"Pretty much," the kids replied together.

Just then Dagon stepped out of the shadows. "I will carry it," his scratchy voice insisted as he reached out to take it from Dr. Paloma.

"No way!" Derek stated as he moved between his father and Dagon, retrieving it from his father's hands. "We will carry it ourselves."

"It is my job," Dagon insisted.

"Not today!" Derek was resolute.

"How did you find it in this dark cave?" Dr. Paloma asked.

Derek and Phoebe responded in unison, "It found us."

AUTHORS NOTE

Dear fellow traveler,

THANK YOU for taking this journey with me. We have traveled over more than thirty-five centuries in time, and the caves have carried us thousands of miles in distance.

Some of you may wonder where the ideas for these stories came from. Are they really in the Bible?

Below I have assembled a brief list of the primary sources for each ancient story. Please check them out and see for yourself. Follow the Crimson Thread of Redemption. It was all written down over 2000 years ago and is waiting for you.

Eden:	*Genesis 3*
Moriah:	*Genesis 22:1-19*
Confrontation:	*Exodus 11*
Passover:	*Exodus 12*
The Other Ark:	*Exodus 25:10-22, Leviticus 16:2, 14-17,*
	Numbers 7:89, Deuteronomy 16:1-8
Qumran:	*Search: Dead Sea Scrolls, Shrine of*
	the Book, Qumran, Israel
The Voice:	*John 3, Isaiah 53,* Psalm 22:1, 16-18
Rahab's Rescue:	Joshua 6
Judgement:	*Luke 22:63-23:15*
Ascent:	*Luke 23:26-54 Matt. 27:50-53*
	Luke 23:45,

Veil: *Hebrews. 10:20, 2 Corinthians 3:16*
                      I Peter 2:9
Emmaus: Luke 24:13-35
Last Red Thread: Hebrews 10:20, 2 Corinthians 3:16,
                      1 Peter 2:9

Additional search suggestions:

Cappadocia, underground cities.
Hagia Sophia, Church of Holy Wisdom, Constantinople
Qumran: Dead Sea Scrolls, Shrine of the Book

A Prayer:

Dear God, I want to know you.
Thank you for sending Jesus, suffering in my place and
dying for what I deserve. I accept your forgiveness, and
open my heart to receive Jesus, my redeemer now.

I, the author, encourage you to add a few of your personal thoughts here….. Let it be. Amen.